thirty
sunsets

thirty sunsets

CHRISTINE HURLEY DERISO

flux®
Woodbury, Minnesota

First Edition
First Printing, 2014

Book design by Bob Gaul
Cover design by Ellen Lawson
Cover image © iStockphoto.com/13733413/UygarGeographic

Flux, an imprint of Llewellyn Worldwide Ltd.

This is a work of fiction. Names, characters, places, and incidents are either the product of the author's imagination or are used fictitiously, and any resemblance to actual persons living or dead, business establishments, events, or locales is entirely coincidental. Cover model used for illustrative purposes only and may not endorse or represent the book's subject.

Library of Congress Cataloging-in-Publication Data
Deriso, Christine Hurley.
  Thirty sunsets/Christine Hurley Deriso.—First edition.
      pages cm
  Summary: "Sixteen-year-old Forrest Shepherd expects to enjoy a relaxing month at her family's beach house, but instead finds herself grappling with a series of relationship crises that lead her to realize things are not always what they seem"—Provided by publisher.
  ISBN 978-0-7387-3991-5
[1. Family life—South Carolina—Fiction. 2. Interpersonal relations—Fiction. 3. Pregnancy—Fiction. 4. Beaches—Fiction. 5. Acquaintance rape—Fiction. 6. Rape—Fiction. 7. South Carolina—Fiction.] I. Title.
  PZ7.D4427Thi 2014
  [Fic]—dc23
                                                        2014009915

Flux
Llewellyn Worldwide Ltd.
2143 Wooddale Drive
Woodbury, MN 55125-2989
www.fluxnow.com

Printed in the United States of America

In memory of my beloved mother, Jane Kamack Hurley, whose soul guides me still.

one

"Hey, Forrest."

I look up from my Faulkner novel and push a lock of windblown hair behind my ear, squinting into the sun.

"Hi."

Play it cool, Forrest. Play it cool.

"Whatcha doin'?"

"Um … " I glance self-consciously at the book on my lap. Darn. The book might as well be a flashing neon sign: *PROPERTY OF GEEK.*

"Is it good?" Jake asks.

"I have to read it for a stupid class," I lie, and hate myself for lying. But, for god's sake, Jake Bennett, a senior, the senior I've had a crush on for two years, is talking to me! To me! Of all the things he could be doing during his lunch period (and why oh why did I pick today to read Faulkner during mine?), he's smiling his adorable grin at *me*!

Jake glances at the space beside me on the bench I've chosen under an oak tree outside the school cafeteria. "Mind if I join you?"

I feel my face flush. "Um … "

Don't blow this, Forrest!

"Sure." I sweep my arm toward the vacant spot in what I intend as a nonchalant do-whatever-floats-your-boat kind of gesture. But my arm sweep is too exaggerated, too clunky, the kind of gesture moms use to get their first grader's attention in the school pick-up line. I'm such a loser.

But Jake sits down anyway, clearing his throat and running his fingers through a tousled lock of hair. His blue eyes sparkle in the balmy spring sunshine.

"So … did you go to the prom last weekend?" he asks me.

Yes. Then I went to the Queen of England's palace for brunch the next day.

"No … " I say, wondering frantically whether that's the right answer. Does not going make me a loser? Or does it signal that I'm available? I can actually hear my heart beating against my T-shirt. "Did you?"

"Yeah," he says. "You didn't miss anything. It was totally lame. The theme was 'Midnight in Paris.' The prom committee makes an Eiffel Tower out of Popsicle sticks, and yeah, I'm totally sold."

I laugh, my heart now actually fluttering. Here I spend the whole year worshipping Jake from a distance based on his studliness, and wonder of wonders, he's wry and sardonic as well!

"So the original isn't made of Popsicle sticks?" I ask, then feel a wave of relief when he laughs.

"You're funny," he says, and the heavens part as I sense that he considers that a good thing.

I gulp, hoping he doesn't notice. This whole exchange is almost too surreal to believe. See, when I started high school last year, I actually thought I had babe potential. With my long blonde hair and hippie figure, people tell me I'm pretty, and my big brother's really cute and popular, so I figured *I've got a decent shot at high school fabulousness, right?* But then I discovered that no, I didn't at all. I was immediately sized up as a brainiac, and if the frizzy-haired president of the friggin' freshman debate team would blow me off (which he did, by the way), then the odds of someone like Jake Bennett noticing me were approximately the same as my dreaming up a cure for cancer en route to picking up my multimillion-dollar lottery prize. I've learned my place.

The rolled eyes of Olivia and the rest of the cheerleading team every time they see me in the hall glued to my brainteaser app have sealed my fate as Sophomore Most Likely to Excel at the Math Meet (which I did, by the way). But now, wonder of wonders, the cutest guy in high school is cutting through all the cliquish crap and seeing me for the incredibly nuanced babe that I am. I *knew* this would happen! My high school fabulosity officially begins *now*.

"So ... who did you go to the prom with?" I ask, aiming for casual.

"Just a bunch of other guys," he says. "I'm totally unattached ... but I'm hoping not for long."

Okay, my heart is now dancing the polka in my chest.

"Yeah?"

He blushes and smiles. "Yeah. See, I hope you don't mind me asking you this, but ... "

"Yeah?" I prod, willing myself not to sound as breathless as I feel.

" ... but I noticed that Brian and Olivia didn't go to the prom."

I stiffen oh-so-slightly.

"Yeah ... ?"

"Right, so, you know, there were rumors that they, like, broke up."

My stomach muscles clench.

Jake's eyes study mine. "So ... did they?"

My eyes narrow. "I'm not my brother's keeper," I say, an edge seeping into my voice.

He furrows his brow. "What? Oh, right. No, I didn't mean that you ... I just thought you might ... oh, hell. You know what? I'm just gonna say it."

Please do. There's still a sliver left of my ego to pulverize.

"See, I've had a crush on Olivia for a while now," he says earnestly, and yup, there goes that last slice of my ego, right into the blender. "I mean, I've dated other girls, but *she* ... " As if on cue, his eyes seem to literally turn into silky puddles of lovesick goo. Adorable.

I clutch my novel tighter, the novel that I'm *not* being

forced to read as a class assignment but that I *choose* to read because I actually have some depth, unlike all the other morons in this godforsaken school, and it's a good thing I love Faulkner since he's apparently the only guy I'll ever hang out with.

"And I'm totally good friends with your brother," Jake continues, "so I would never in a million years screw that up, but if Brian and Olivia *are* officially broken up, then . . . "

I guess I'm staring into space. " . . . and I didn't want to ask Brian," Jake blathers on, to fill the awkward silence, "because, well, you know, it's kind of sensitive, and he's seemed really bummed lately, so . . . "

Another pause, one that I'm evidently expected to fill.

"They're still a couple," I say simply.

"Oh."

Jake rubs his hands together, and I guess I could fill this awkward silence too, saying something cheerful or funny or consoling or cajoling or what-the-hell-ever.

Except that I don't. I'm done with this conversation.

"*Sooo* . . . okay," Jake says, rising from the bench, clearly hoping we've shared the last nanosecond that he will ever have to suffer through again. "Got it. And, hey, Brian and I are totally cool. I just thought . . . well . . . hey, enjoy your book."

Two weeks. There are two weeks left of my sophomore year at Peachfield High School. After so many months of disappointments, humiliations, mortifications, and general crapfests, who would have guessed that my nadir would come so late in the year? Assuming this *is* the nadir. After all, I have two weeks to go ... then two more years of high school after *that*.

Perhaps my slow slog through Loserville has only just begun.

two

"O-M-Geeee!" Shelley says in a singsong voice, nudging me aside as she plops next to me on the bench, her strawberry-blonde ponytail bouncing as she settles in. "Was Jake Bennett just talking to *you*?"

"Yeah, we're engaged now."

Shelley pokes me with her elbow. "Tell me what he said!"

I shut my book and sigh. "Am I, like, hideous?"

Shelley raises an eyebrow. "He told you that you're hideous?"

I shrug. "He asked if Brian and Olivia are still together. But I think the unspoken upshot was, 'Oh, by the way, you're hideous.'"

"What *is* up with those two?" Shelley asks, biting into an apple. "I heard they didn't even go to the prom."

"Yeah, I alerted the media."

Shelley eyes me warily. "Wanna hear the rumors?"

I roll my eyes. Brian and Olivia have garnered significantly more than their fifteen minutes of Peachfield High School fame since they started dating last summer. Their adorableness is apparently too precious to go unchronicled by the school wannabes, and the tongue-wagging went into overdrive when they blew off the prom. I'm starting to feel more like Brian's publicist than his sister.

"You know I don't do gossip," I remind Shelley.

"Oh please."

I wrinkle my nose at her. Shelley's been by my side since third grade to blow holes in my above-it-all attitude. Only *she* knows that I crush on cute seniors and harbor secret cravings to be invited to lame proms featuring Eiffel Towers made of Popsicle sticks. She knows I'd rather be in the game than on the sidelines mocking those who have somehow learned how to successfully nail it. She knows it, but it's our little secret. I love that about her.

"The *rumor*," Shelley continues conspiratorially, "is that Brian still totally loves Olivia but can't bear to watch her destroy herself with her bulimia, so, you know, he's taking a break. The whole tough-love thing."

I bristle. "Who says she's bulimic?"

"Uh, *duh*," Shelley says. "She barfs after lunch, like, every day. And have you noticed how skinny she's gotten?"

My back stiffens. I'm not exactly president of the Olivia fan club, but that doesn't mean I want people being snarky behind her back.

Shelley studies my scowl and says, "Whatevs. *You're* the one who hates her for being your brother's girlfriend."

See, that's the thing: I don't hate her because she's my brother's girlfriend. How petty and neurotic and borderline creepy would *that* be? I hated her *before* she was my brother's girlfriend, and for totally legitimate reasons. I still remember the day I walked into chorus practice in a romper and she curled a lip at me. I know, a romper, what was I thinking? But god, did that curled lip sear my soul. I've been shlumping around in sweats, jeans, and T-shirts ever since.

Then there was the time I saw Olivia at a football game with some pretty blonde who looked just like her. I asked if they were sisters, and both of their jaws dropped. When I walked away, I heard this crazed hyena laughter echoing through the bleachers. I found out afterward that the "sister" was Olivia's mother. Hysterical, huh? It was such a thrill to know my idiocy made their day.

It's that kind of thing that makes my stomach clench when Olivia crosses my path. Throw in the factoid that she derailed my brother's college plans and I think I've got a pretty fair claim to an attitude. But I'm not the kind of petty, neurotic, borderline-creepy person who hates my brother's girlfriends just on principle. Olivia earned it.

Still, I'm way too cool to let her know she gets under my skin. (My romper days are over.)

"Hey, are you coming to Bri's graduation?" I ask, eager to change the subject. "Mom is having some people over to the house afterward."

"Oooohh, is she making her gooey butter bars?" Shelley asks.

"I'll put in your order."

"I'm in. I've got to fill my quota before you abandon me this summer."

I jab her lightly with my elbow. "You know you're always welcome at our beach house."

I wince at how pretentious I just sounded, and Shelley notices right away.

"Oh, *please* can I come to Spackle Beach?" she teases, pressing her palms in prayer position. "You'll never even know I'm there; I'll hole up in the east wing and have your butler bring me table scraps."

I sputter with laughter. Yes, it sounds nauseatingly Kardashian-esque to lay claim to a "beach house," but Shelley's been there enough to know that it's strictly no-frills. The butler, for instance, is only there on weekdays. (Just kidding. We don't have a butler.)

And yes, it's on an island (a huge draw for us residents of landlocked Peachfield, South Carolina, a boring orchard grove turned mill town turned computer-parts mecca housing all of forty thousand people), but that's where the glamour begins and ends. The actual name of the island is Sparkle Beach; Brian and I renamed it as a shout-out to Mom's badger-like tenacity, which in this case worked to our advantage.

Dad usually lets Mom have her way, but he put his foot down when she decided that we needed a beach house. Too expensive, too impractical, too much of a flood risk, too indulgent ("Do you want our kids to be spoiled rotten?!?")—he lobbed all of his most trusty artillery.

But Mom lobbed right back: it would be an investment. We'd never spend another dime on a hotel, cruise ship, or amusement park. Think of the tax breaks! The kids are only young once.

Dad probably would have stood his ground, but in addition to Mom's arguments, her ace in the hole was having Brian and me jump up and down like banshees pleading her case. (We were happy to oblige.)

We finally wore Dad down, but with the caveat that we would not spend one more red cent on that &#*$ house than was absolutely necessary. We'd furnish it with our old tattered sofa and squeaky recliner; we'd decorate it with Brian's and my crappy art projects; we'd eat peanut butter sandwiches morning, noon, and night.

"Fine, fine!" we'd all squealed, scooping each other off the floor in ecstasy. *Our own beach house!* I'd never felt so deliciously elite in my life.

Mom's been a good sport about making good on her end of the bargain. When Brian knocked over a space heater and seared a hole in the house's family room carpet, Mom tossed an area rug on top of it. When I splattered nail polish on the wall, she hung a mirror to cover it, even though it was way lower than the eye-level height she prefers. When the tattered sofa started literally bursting at the seams, she flung a slipcover over it.

So we dubbed it the Spackle Beach House. Looks great at a glance, but things get dicey if you dig just beneath the surface.

"*Come,*" I cajole Shelley.

"You'll be there in June?"

"Right, the whole month. We're leaving a couple of days after Bri's graduation. We'll even upgrade you to the *west* wing this summer, if you'd like."

She gives an exaggerated pout. "I gotta work at my aunt's office this summer."

I squinch up my face disapprovingly. "The veterinarian?"

She huffs. "Yes, Forrest. I'll be cleaning out litter boxes while you loll on the beach. Thanks for making sure we're both abundantly clear on that point."

I narrow my eyes at her playfully, then turn wistful. "At least we'll be away from *her* for a while. Maybe I can make Brian come to his senses once he has a little distance from her. I mean, *Starrett Community College?* He's planned on studying pre-med at Vanderbilt since he was, like, in the womb, then Olivia breezes into his life and it's like, 'Welding school, here I come.'"

The bell rings, and Shelley and I rise from the bench as other students start filing past us en route to their next class.

"I like welders," she says cheerfully as she hoists her backpack onto her shoulders, tossing her apple core into a nearby trash can. "But not as much as I like gooey butter bars. Remind your mom: gooey butter bars."

I tuck my Faulkner novel into my backpack.

"Right. Gooey butter bars."

three

"The *crudités*, Forrest, the *crudités*."

Mom's voice is a whisper, but it's a Significant Whisper, an I'm-asking-you-for-the-last-time-to-refill-the-gosh-darn-crudité-tray whisper.

Then she turns around and gives an exaggerated smile to Aunt Faye.

"More crudités, coming up!" she says brightly, and really, just how desperate is Aunt Faye (or anyone else, for that matter) for more crudités?

But I slog to the kitchen anyway. Mom's type-A personality goes into overdrive when she's playing hostess, and she's been anal for a full two weeks about Brian's graduation party.

Bri is walking out of the kitchen as I walk in, licking gooey butter bar icing from his fingers. He's changed from his graduation garb into shorts and a T-shirt, but he's wearing his honors tassel around his neck. I'd joked to him before the ceremony that I planned to count how many times Mom worked the fact that he's an honors student into conversation throughout the evening, so he tugs on the tassel as an inside joke.

"*Fourteen*," I mouth, but truly, she's probably mentioned it twice that many times by now. I've stopped counting, because now I'm on crudité patrol.

I open the fridge and grab baggies of crisp baby carrots, cucumbers, celery sticks, and green peppers, then walk them back out to the buffet table. Mom gives me a wide-eyed look of alarm from across the room, as in *OMG, don't you know you're supposed to take the tray to the kitchen rather than the baggies to the buffet table?*

I drop my jaw and arch my brows in mock horror, as in *OMG, Mom, how will I ever make this up to you?*

Mom giggles into her fingertips in spite of herself, then resumes her conversation with Aunt Faye as I dump the veggies onto the tray.

As crazy as Mom drives me, I'm really happy to see her smile. She's been hugely tense lately, and not just because she's in hostess mode.

She's even more anti-Olivia than I am, and it killed her when Brian blew off Vanderbilt. I was the one who broke the news to her. I'd watched him open his acceptance letter in the kitchen one day after school a few months earlier, read it like it was a credit card offer, then toss it into the garbage can along with the empty Snickers wrapper he was holding.

"What?" he'd asked blandly when he saw my expression.

"That was from Vandy, right?" I said.

He nodded.

"Well? Did you get in?"

He shrugged. "Yeah ... "

I flung my hands in the air. "Then you're going, idiot!"

Brian smiled indulgently, a dimple burrowing into his left cheek. "You can have my spot."

I lurched toward him, grabbing his shoulders. "You are not blowing off college for her!"

The smile held steady, but his eyes turned slightly flinty. His message was clear: *I'm keeping my cool, Forrest, but drop it.*

But I couldn't drop it. It was one thing when he was just *intimating* a change in plans. It was another to toss his acceptance letter into the trash can, staining it with Snickers.

"For *her*?" I practically shrieked. "For that *bimbo*? Her own *mother* flaked out on her, Brian!"

And that's when his gaze hardened. He shook his shoulders roughly to dislodge my hands. "Talk about her like that again," he said steadily, "and we're done."

Then he turned and walked away.

I literally shivered. My knees buckled. My palm opened in front of me, a pathetic proffer to the gods to hand me a way to fix this.

Done? Can a brother and sister be *done*? We hadn't even talked like that when we were kids fighting over the Pogs in our Alpha-Bits.

But if I'd had any doubt before, I didn't any more. He would choose her over me if he had to. Geez, he was choosing her over *college*, which was almost even worse. Brian had talked about medical school since he was in kindergarten. Sure, Mom had planted the seed, but it *took*, you know? He really is scary-good at math and science. He really does love examining every disgusting bug in the park. He grills our family doctor about the exact nature of whatever virus is making his ear ache. He was meant to be a doctor, and Vanderbilt had always been his dream.

Until *she* came along.

His hints were subtle at first: "Big universities are a total rip-off," or "I could get my core courses right here in town," or "I like my part-time landscaping job a lot more than I thought I would." Mom's hands would ball into fists when Brian would say something like that, the back of her neck turning scarlet. But Brian had apparently given *her* the come-to-Jesus lecture too, so she would hold her tongue and hope it was just a phase, that Olivia was just a fling, that she'd soon have a Vandy bumper sticker on her car.

Then, *poof*. Even as he was nailing his finals and basking in his stellar SAT scores, he was informing us that his decision was final: he was enrolling in Starrett Community College in the fall, clearly to stay close to Luscious Liv.

Mom and I disagree over just about every conceivable topic, but even though we've learned to keep our mouths shut around Brian, we're totally on the same page regarding Olivia's she-devil status.

Speaking of whom . . .

Olivia sidles up to the buffet table and grabs a celery

stick. She flashes me a conciliatory smile (she's fake-nice to me around Brian) and says, "Delicious."

Is she being sarcastic? I mean, can a celery stick truly be delicious?

She flips her long blonde hair and it cascades over her shoulder. Several out-of-town guests at the party have commented that we look like sisters, and I've made a mental note to pull my hair into a ponytail to nip the comparisons in the bud, but I haven't gotten around to it yet.

I'm tempted to follow up on the celery-is-delicious thread, but I'm on my best behavior tonight, so I change the subject instead. "Are your parents here?" I ask.

Olivia swallows a bite of the celery stick. "My dad."

"Oh. Where's your mom?"

Okay, I *swear* I didn't mean to sound snarky. It truly slipped my mind for a second that her mom bailed on her and her dad years ago and they hardly ever see her. But *surely* she came to her daughter's graduation ... right? I feel a stab of pity as Olivia's eyes fall.

"She was going to come," she murmurs, "but ... "

An awkward moment hangs in the air.

"Hey," I say, "my mom is annoying enough for, like, *seven* mothers, so I think we've got that base covered."

Olivia swallows hard, but brightens when she sees a fellow cheerleader, Casey, walking toward us.

"Hey, girl!" Olivia gushes, and they hug and give air kisses.

"Did you see that Shelley girl over there?" Casey says in

Olivia's ear. "She's wearing a strapless dress! Can I commit a random act of kindness by informing her that a strapless dress requires boobs larger than golf balls?"

Casey presses her fingers against her mouth as she laughs at her cleverness.

"Shelley's my best friend," I say.

"Oh..." Casey stammers, clearly noticing me for the first time. "I didn't mean..."

"And, oh look, I'm wearing a strapless dress too. Maybe you can commit two random acts of kindness in one night."

Casey freezes momentarily, then says, "*You* look great in it. And Shelley does too. I was *kidding*, silly!"

I observe her coolly.

"Um... Olivia, come say hi to my mom," Casey says, pulling her forearm. They flash fake smiles at me and scurry away.

"Supercilious."

I turn and face Dad, who's just walked up to me biting into a chip. He likes to randomly throw vocabulary words at me—he's a magazine editor—and I pathetically enjoy it, mostly because he almost never trips me up.

"The inability to get over one's fabulous self," I respond. "Use it in a sentence, you say? 'Olivia and her A-list friends are revoltingly supercilious.'"

Dad smiles, his eyes twinkling. "They're not so bad. I'm really getting to like Olivia."

I raise an eyebrow.

"Ouch," he says. "That's your mother's look."

I dig my nails into my palms. "I give her and Brian three more months, tops. Now that she's concluded her illustrious stint as head cheerleader, I think she's officially peaked. Unless there's a big demand for cartwheels in the real world."

Dad tousles my hair. "C'mon, Smokey, give her a chance," he says, choosing one of a million forest-related nicknames he calls me based on whatever pops into his head at the time.

Granted, Dad is a give-folks-a-chance kind of guy, but he knows as well as I do that Olivia is solely responsible for his future *My Son, the Welder* bumper sticker.

Shelley walks over to us and Dad gives her a bear hug. "You look beautiful," he tells her.

"Like a rock star," I add, "and I *love* your dress."

"Oh, wow," she says, and curtsies.

Give Olivia a chance? I think. *Fat chance.*

four

"So much for rumors."

"What do you mean?" I ask Shelley as we round the corner of the mall.

"Well, it was obvious at the graduation party last night that Brian and Olivia are still a couple," Shelley says. "Wonder why they blew off the prom."

We walk into a boutique and I start rummaging through a rack of polka-dot spandex bras and barely there bikini bottoms, not because I would ever wear one but because it's the first rack I pass. I'd normally prefer coal-mining to shopping, but our beach trip starts tomorrow and I've grown three inches since last summer, so...

I pull a teal bikini closer and squeeze the fabric between my fingertips.

"Oooohh, that's adorable!" Shelley coos. "Try it on."

I furrow my brow. "You can't be serious."

"Of course I'm serious! I mean, I wouldn't have expected you to like it, but since you're looking…"

Okay, I've got my reputation to consider. I walk away from the bikinis and head for the rack of Speedos.

"Forrest Shepherd, you are *not* wearing a Speedo on the beach," Shelley scolds in my wake. "Speedos are for swim meets."

But I'm already thumbing through the rack of one-piece racerbacks.

"Is it out of the question to meet a hot guy at the beach?" Shelley whines. "Or, I dunno, maybe actually go out on a *date*? God, you might as well skip the rest of high school and head directly for a convent."

"In my Speedo?" I ask blithely without looking up from the price tag I'm checking.

"That would be an improvement over the sweats you normally shlump through school in. And you've got such a great body! Geez, no wonder we spend Saturday nights watching the Biography Channel."

I check a price tag. "Don't hold me responsible for your social life or lack thereof."

"Uh, hello? I've had *four boyfriends* already."

I smile mischievously. "Remember the one you had to drive to his orthodontist appointments? What was his name—Waldo? I think his disgusting retainer is still in your mom's glove compartment. Good thing he moved, or you'd be reminding him to floss."

"Hey, we're still Facebook friends, and he's gotten really cute," Shelley protests. "*Walden*, by the way. Oh, and he's a *musician*."

I look at her evenly. "He plays the bagpipes."

"Yeah, well, get Boyfriend Number One in the pipeline and we'll talk."

Shelley glances toward the entrance to the store and her eyes widen. I follow her gaze and see Olivia coming inside. Olivia catches my eye, freezes for a nanosecond, obviously deduces it's too late to walk back out, and offers a little wave.

"Hi," I say coolly as she approaches us, still stung from the way she and her moron friend talked about Shelley the night before. Well, I guess technically it was the friend who did the talking, but still…

"Hi. Buying a new bathing suit for the beach?" Olivia asks me, fingering the necklace that shimmers against her bronzed skin.

"Yeah…"

"Me too," she says.

Oh.

Wait, what?

"You've got a beach trip coming up?" I ask.

Olivia blushes. "I thought you knew," she says, her hand fumbling over her peach-glossed lips.

"Knew that you were going to the beach?" I ask.

"Yeah…"

"Why would I know about your beach trip?"

Awkward pause.

Oh. Because *her* beach trip is *my* beach trip.

This can't be happening.

"I hope it's okay," she mumbles, her fingers still hiding her mouth.

Shelley's eyebrows arch. "Oh! *You're* going with *her*," she helpfully points out. "How... awesome."

"For the whole month?" I ask, knowing it sounds rude but I'm still trying to grasp what an astonishingly miserable turn my summer has suddenly taken.

"Your mom says there's plenty of room." My rudeness has apparently registered, because a touch of haughtiness now factors into Olivia's voice. She pulls her hand away from her mouth and plants it into the back pocket of her cutoffs, standing a little straighter and arching her eyebrow ever so slightly. *Deal with it, bitch.*

"So no biggie if I come along too?" Shelley asks, then laughs gamely at herself upon realizing that Olivia and I are too busy boring holes into each other's eyes to appreciate her humor. "Fun summer. Good times."

"Your mother invited me," Olivia says, like this is somehow supposed to strike me as persuasive or relevant in any way whatsoever.

"Did she."

Olivia holds the frosty gaze for a second longer, then sighs. "I really hope we can have a good time."

I try to utter an appropriate response, but the only thought coursing through my brain is the one that has occupied 90 percent of my gray cells since puberty: *I am going to kill my mother.*

five

"I could have sworn I mentioned it."

Mom doesn't bother to look up from packing as she utters these insanity-inducing words.

I dig my nails into my palms. "No, you didn't mention it."

"Do you want me to pack your beach towels?" she asks.

I move from the doorway into the bedroom and pound my fist against her floral bedspread, making the suitcase jump.

"Oh, quit being so dramatic," Mom mutters, adding some neatly folded beach towels onto the top of the pile.

Dad walks in the room and ruffles my hair. "'Sup, Redwood."

"Did you know Olivia is coming with us to Spackle Beach?" I ask him.

"Nope."

There's no satisfaction in his answer whatsoever, because

he doesn't care. Mom could invite the Mormon Tabernacle Choir and he would blissfully roll with the punches.

"Well, *neither did I.*"

"There's enough ocean for both of you," Mom says breezily, which is even more condescending than it sounds simply because she *knows* condescension drives me over the edge.

"Hey, Mom, are you packing beach towels for Olivia and me?"

We look toward the door and see Brian walking in, his loose curls spilling out from underneath his baseball cap.

"Yup," Mom answers him. "Beach towels for everybody."

I exchange furtive glances with my parents.

"What?" Brian asks me, narrowing his eyes.

"Nothing." I offer a peace sign and walk out of the room.

I go into my room, close the door behind me, and plop facedown onto my bed. I've learned my lesson: no Olivia-bashing around Brian. But does being civil require inviting her to the beach? For a *month,* no less? What was Mom *thinking?*

I squeeze the plump, cool comforter between my fingers, then feel my lashes flutter. It's only mid-afternoon, but I was up late last night washing dishes long after the last guest had left Brian's graduation party, then Shelley and I got an early start at the mall this morning, then I found out my summer's ruined (how exhausting is *that*), and I'm really, really sleepy, and...

"... and don't forget my rash cream."

"I won't forget," I tell Brian before running to the store, which is what my kitchen transforms into in my dream.

Brian started breaking out in weird rashes a few months earlier, and three trips to the dermatologist haven't helped. I tell Brian I've just seen a great new product advertised on an infomercial, which I'll be glad to trot down to the store to get him if he'd like.

So I go to the store/kitchen and rummage through cabinets until I find the cream, which has a picture of a smiley face on it, then beam that I've finally solved my brother's problem. But the grocery guy tells me, "Whoa, hold everything, not just anybody can purchase this new miracle cream," but I explain that my brother isn't just anybody, he's the best brother and most amazing guy you'll ever meet, and nothing else is helping his rashes, so he really, really needs this miracle cream, and...

"Okay, okay," Grocery Guy finally says, but he tells me in a somber tone to be careful; a little goes a long way. So I buy it, then skip from the store/kitchen to Brian's bedroom and announce I've solved his problem. He looks skeptical, but I'm so thrilled that I open the jar myself and start slathering it on his face.

Uh-oh... I thought I was helping, but damn if that "little goes a long way" admonition wasn't an understatement, because chunks of his face start falling off.

Too much! I've helped too much! The rash is gone, but so are his cheeks! His bones are jutting out, and he doesn't even realize it yet. One of his eyes is starting to droop as the flesh underneath falls away. Brian totally trusted me as I slathered this crap on his face, and now his face is falling off, and OMG, wait till he sees, and what was I thinking, I was just trying to help, really I was ...

———————

I wake in a cold sweat and glance at the clock on my bedside table.

Only twenty minutes have passed since I dozed off—long enough to have another weird dream about Brian. I've been having them a lot lately. Sure, I've always had the occasional dream about my brother, but for the past few months they've taken on a jarring intensity and horror-show quality.

What's up with that? It's true I've been extra worried about him since he blew off Vandy, but that's not all it is. Something deeper is nagging at me.

There's something I don't know.

I push myself off the bed and shudder, suddenly chilled.

Yes, I'm sure of it. Even though my sixth sense is too vague and sketchy to discuss without risking making a fool of myself, I totally trust it. I've always had a connection to Brian that clues me in when something's wrong. I can *feel* it.

There's definitely something I don't know.

six

"Sorry. You go."

"No, you."

"No, really…"

I don't have the energy for another round of which one of us gets the seat belt clasp that Olivia and I have both inadvertently laid claim to. I let go of my seat belt buckle and watch the strap get sucked back into the seat.

"Put your seat belt on," Brian tells me testily as Olivia, sitting in between us in the back seat, primly buckles up. "You were using the wrong clasp."

I toss my hand dismissively in Brian's direction, then turn toward the window, press my pillow against it, and settle in for a welcome bout of unconsciousness as Dad backs the car out of the driveway.

I guess my vibes are frosty enough to put everyone on notice, because no one, not even my neurotic mother, reiterates the demand for me to buckle my seat belt. Mom can only push her luck so far, you know: first I get blindsided with the news that I'll be sharing a beach house with OMG-livia for a month, then I get sardined by her side for the three-hour car ride. Apparently Mom is willing to take her chances that Dad will drive safely enough to avoid flinging me onto the pavement.

I feel Olivia inch as far away from me as possible, but how far can she go without climbing into Brian's lap? It must drive her nuts that our thighs will be plastered together for the next hundred-and-fifty miles. With her poof-tastic ponytail, hint-o-blush rosy glow, and painted-on Daisy Dukes, I'm guessing that intermingled thigh sweat is a Fashion Don't.

From the front seat, Mom cranes her neck in my direction long enough to shoot me a Significant Glance. Until recently, Olivia's Daisy Dukes alone would have been cause for a convulsive round of throat-clearing and brow-furrowing, but suddenly *I'm* the problem. I don't know what caused Mom's change of heart. A new reading of the Riot Act by Brian? A particularly home-hitting episode of Dr. Phil? An attack of conscience? (Mom has fretted before that Olivia desperately needs a mother figure.) Who knows. But for whatever reason, Mom is definitely aboard the O-train now, and O seems to sense it, squeezing Brian's hand possessively as Dad cruises down the street and heads for the interstate.

I punch my pillow and plug in my earbuds. Elliott Smith's plaintive song fills my head as my eyelashes flutter shut: "Going Nowhere."

"Get Mom."

Brian's voice is calm despite the blood streaming in rivulets down his cheeks. The gash on his head has already matted his brown curls. His gold-flecked eyes are solemn but stoic; he holds my gaze, no doubt sensing that if I look away, I'll crumple to the ground.

That can't happen. The greenway is pretty isolated right now; Brian and I got an early start this Saturday morning to walk the path to the riverbank in search of arrowheads, and no one's in sight right now. An hour from now, a steady stream of bikers, skaters, and runners will fill the path, but our only current company is a bird chirping overhead, its perky tune sounding downright sadistic in light of the carnage below.

The greenway was built over train tracks, and this section is a ravine with steep, jagged granite on either side. It was typical of Brian to opt for a leisurely journey to the riverbank—I'm more of a direct-to-destination kinda girl—so I was already tromping well ahead of him when I heard him scream. I spun around and saw him lying face down on the pavement a hundred or so yards behind me. He'd clearly attempted what he'd done a hundred times before—shimmying up the rock as far as he could go before lowering himself, foothold by tenuous foothold, back to the greenway—only this time, he'd fast-forwarded the trip back down, apparently twisting around in midair and falling onto his chest.

As I ran toward him, my eyes blurry with tears, I saw the

gash on his forehead. His palms and knees were bloody and gravel-flecked too. By the time I reached him, he'd lifted himself up, then flopped backward onto his butt, dazed but steady. Brian's always steady.

Mom. Get Mom.

So I'm running to get her, and here's where things get weird, because in real life, six years earlier, I'd actually done just that—gotten Mom—and Brian was in the emergency room by the time Scooby-Doo was on. But now, in my dream, and even though I'm vaguely aware it's a dream but am still terrified as crap, I get home, then forget to tell Mom about the crisis I've rushed home to report. Instead, I go about the urgent business of a ten-year-old on a Saturday morning, which mostly involves going to Shelley's house three doors down and playing Barbies. Hours pass before I realize OMG, I forgot all about Brian and he's lying there bleeding and I was supposed to get Mom, and OMG OMG, how many hours have passed and is he even still alive and will he ever forgive me and how can I ever make this up to him and . . .

"Forrest!"

"I'm coming, Brian!" I cry as I race back onto the greenway.

"Forrest! Forrest . . . "

"Forrest!"

My eyes open slowly, my head still pressed against the window of the car.

"Forrest!" Brian repeats.

"What..." I mumble.

"Time for breakfast," he says.

My eyes squint against the white-hot morning sun. I blink a couple of times and sit up straighter to survey the Golden Arches we're approaching.

Dad pulls into a parking space. Even as we pile out of the car, I can't shake the dream and keep glancing at Brian for confirmation that he's alive and well.

"Wait *up*," Olivia tells him with a pout as we head inside. But instead of putting her prissy ass in gear to catch up with Brian, she puts a hand on her hip and plants her feet. Brian has no choice but to turn back around to collect her. He sheepishly trots to her side, then takes her hand and leads her inside.

That's right, bro: she's got you moving backward. It'll be the story of your life if you stay with this princess.

I need to pee, but Olivia heads for the bathroom when we get inside, so I'll wait.

"Put your seat belt on when we get back in the car," Brian mutters as we stand in line, and you know what? I'm touched. It's been driving him crazy that I've logged a hundred miles without a seat belt.

"Yes, Forrest," Mom chimes in, craning her neck to get a better look at the menu in case oh, I dunno, McDonald's has suddenly started serving brioche. "I insist you wear your seat belt." Now that's just annoying.

Olivia emerges from the bathroom and sidles up against Brian.

"Whatcha want, baby?" Brian coos, and omigod is this gonna be a long month.

"Ummmmm…" She holds a French-manicured fingertip against her plump bottom lip. "Do you think they have yogurt?"

Her lashes flutter as she looks up at him, all baby-blue-eyed preciousness, and it occurs to me to direct her attention to the menu, but really, who could bear to spoil this adorable Kodak moment?

"They have parfaits," Mom tells her, breaking the spell. If Olivia hasn't learned by now that Mom is the ultimate buzz-kill, well, there's no time like the present.

"Do you like parfaits?" Mom persists, just in case Olivia isn't yet clear that intimate moments will be hard to come by for the next few weeks.

But Olivia keeps gazing into Brian's eyes (you've got to give her props for at least *trying* to blow Mom off, and good luck with that), conveying some kind of subliminal message that it's now his responsibility to translate to us.

"She'd rather have plain yogurt," he tells us, as solemnly as if announcing that North Korea has opted for democracy.

"Well, all you have to do is spoon off the fruit," Mom says, a subdued hint of *ya gotta be kidding me* flashing across her face. "Or just eat around it."

Olivia's urgent eye contact with Brian is still speaking volumes.

"I'll take care of it," Brian says, and now it's our turn to order, so he's asking a polyester-clad teenager if she can hold the fruit on Preciousness's yogurt.

The teenager looks confused, so Brian leans into the counter to more fully explain why he's giving her something besides a friggin' number, seeing as *this is McDonald's* for crying out loud.

Olivia, of course, hangs back, not wanting to suffer through the tedious details of her specialized McDonald's order. *Just give me what I want,* her pouty, dismissive expression seems to convey, and against all odds I have no doubt that fruit-free yogurt will soon emerge, miraculously, from Brian's loving hands.

Having never had an actual boyfriend, I briefly ponder what it would be like to have some sap fawning over me, granting my every desire, arranging for a fruit-free parfait upon command, and truthfully this scenario would make me gag even if I were on the receiving end of this Bounty of Love.

"Fruit's good for you, you know," Mom says under her breath, no longer able to withhold her disdain.

"Olivia likes cantaloupe," Brian says as the rest of us place lowly, uncomplicated orders. "Mom, can you make sure we have lots of cantaloupe at the beach house?"

I'm tempted to volunteer my interpretative dance skills for Olivia's entertainment at the beach house, should that be to her liking, but now I'm too hungry to be catty. Olivia's order has caused quite a stir among the McDonald's staff, with lots of murmuring and scuttling about involved. We may not eat for another forty minutes at this rate. Damn her fruit-free parfait!

Mom is doing that Cher thing where she runs her tongue slowly along the outline of her mouth, but whereas this gesture makes Cher look sexy, it makes Mom look homicidal. She's gripping her arms across her chest and digging her fingernails into her flesh. It seems entirely possible that her head might explode. *Still lovin' on Olivia, Mom? Still thinking it was a swell idea to invite her to our beach house for a month?*

Dad is whistling "Take Me Out to the Ballgame." Nothing rains on Dad's parade. You gotta love that about him.

The food eventually materializes (Brian looks insanely pleased to present Olivia her fruit-free parfait), and we settle glumly into a bright-yellow booth. Brian and Olivia share one side, or rather I should say that Brian, Olivia, and her huge Prada bag share one side. I sit on the other with Dad, Mom, and Mom's fanny pack.

I wolf down my food, casting furtive glances toward Olivia as she takes dainty bites, wrapping her luscious lips around a plastic spoon turned arch-side up. Is there anything normal about this girl?

Dad is sharing the five-day forecast he's committed to memory, noting the pros and cons of scattered afternoon thundershowers (a shame if we get chased off the beach early, but if we hit the showers by four p.m., we'll have a good chance of catching an early bird special), and I'm playing trivia on my smartphone. The question is how many times the Beatles say "yeah" in "She Loves You," so I'm singing the song in my head and counting the "yeahs" on my fingers. Olivia curls her lip at me.

Yeah, sugarlips, I'm the weird one.

Then Olivia suddenly springs to her feet. "Restroom," she says, her eyes widening.

Brian jumps up. "Do you need help?" he asks as she bolts past him, and my imagination would go into overdrive wondering how he might help her in the restroom except that I'm too busy counting "yeahs."

Thirty, I type into my phone.

Wrong. Twenty-nine. Twenty-nine "yeahs."

"What's the matter with her?" I ask absently, still staring at my phone.

"Nothing's the matter with her," Brian snaps, and don't think it's going unnoticed how much he snaps at me lately.

Then *my* eyes widen.

Maybe it's true, that whole bulimia rumor.

I'm tempted to text Shelley—*Olivia just bolted to the bathroom after finishing her breakfast!*—but Mom's always looking over my shoulder and besides, I really meant what I said about not liking to dish dirt, so it's just as well that I continue my trivia game while Dad moves on to day four of the five-day forecast.

Let's see: How many five-day forecasts will factor into our beach trip? My heart sinks at the answer (and this one I get right): six. Six five-day forecasts.

I used to love every minute of our trips to Spackle Beach,

but that fruit-free parfait has wreaked serious havoc on my attitude.

It's gonna be a long month.

seven

Salt.

I sniff deeper.

Yep. We're here.

I open my eyes, groggily sit up straighter, and look out the window. Palm trees. Crepe myrtle. Sea gulls.

We're on Spackle Beach.

I love this place ... a tiny, perfect little slice of heaven. When we first started coming here when I was little, it was quiet and pristine. Now that the tourists have discovered it, it's cramped and congested.

But still beautiful. The island enforces strict codes regulating things like architecture and signage. No billboards are allowed on Spackle Beach; even signs outside stores have to be discreet and downsized; unless you know the island like the back of your hand, you can't tell where a restaurant or gas station is until you're right in front of it. No towering golden arches on Spackle Beach. Everything that God himself hasn't erected on the island is tucked into the background as unobtrusively as possible.

That's why, even though a zillion floppy-hatted tourists now roam the island on car, foot, boat, and bicycle, it still looks lush and tropical. I feel a rush of exhilaration every time we cross the gleaming, mile-long bridge connecting the mainland to the island.

We're crossing that bridge now.

Once we're on the island, we ease unconsciously into tourist time. Dad slows the car to a crawl as sunburned people in bathing suits, shorts, and flip-flops ride bikes, jog on paths adjacent to the highway, or trot across the street lugging rafts, beach chairs, and coolers. Dad whistles along with the radio as Mom retrieves a to-do list from her purse, scanning it hastily. She'll whip out her cleaning supplies within nanoseconds of pulling into the driveway of our house. Occasionally she'll assign a few chores to the rest of us, but nobody can scrub a tub or mop a floor or dust a room like Mom, so, hey, what are you gonna do.

We turn onto a bougainvillea-lined street, then take another right, then pass one house, then another, then another . . . and here we are. I can hear the ocean even from the driveway.

Dad parks the car, pops the trunk, and starts handing us luggage. Bri's the first one to the front door. He fumbles with the key for a second, turns it, and lets the door swing open wide.

We pile in behind him, and I breathe in the two-month

accumulation of mustiness that will soon be replaced with pine-scented disinfectant. I scan the house from the foyer. Even Mom on a budget makes things prettier than most interior decorators could manage with a blank check. Scarlet-red and lemon-yellow pillows accent overstuffed sofas in the great room. Cozy afghans are draped casually over chairs. Gleaming utensils hang from the kitchen ceiling. And you know those hideous things people make with stuff from the beach, like seashell lampshades? Mom does that too, but with inexplicably classy, pretty results.

But the biggest draw is the floor-to-ceiling windows against the back of the house, revealing an OMG view of the Atlantic Ocean. The redwood cedar deck that runs the length of the house is a perfect place to sleep in the fall and spring.

I'd eat peanut butter sandwiches for the rest of my friggin' life to be here.

We're at Spackle Beach.

We're home.

eight

"Top or bottom?"

Say *what*?

Why did it not occur to me that Olivia and I would be sharing a room? Up until this morning, the news that she would be joining us on our beach trip seemed kinda, I don't know, conceptual. Like if you win a date with a movie star and spend so much time chewing over the very *idea* of it that you never give a thought to the details until there you are, sitting in a restaurant with a stranger, wondering what on God's green earth to talk about.

Where did I *think* Olivia would sleep? I don't know, I don't know ... I guess I just couldn't envision her in a bunk bed. Yet here she is.

"Top, if you don't mind," I say.

She nods. "That's fine."

"I mean, if you *want* the top bunk ... "

"No, no, the bottom one's fine. I'll be able to get to the bathroom easier."

I start transferring clothes from my suitcase into the dresser as I ponder her need for unfettered bathroom access.

"I love Brian, you know."

Whoa. Where did that *come from?*

"What?" I ask, even though I'm clear on what Olivia just said.

"I love Brian. I want you to know that."

As I face her, holding a pile of folded T-shirts, I try to read her expression. Is this a challenge, an *in your face* declaration of her territory? Is it a truce, a *we have nothing in common but we both love Brian so pass the sunscreen and let's move on* kind of moment? I have no idea, and Olivia's face is inscrutable. With her Bambi eyes and plump, moist lips, maybe she's too pretty to look anything but bland.

Or maybe she likes being inscrutable. Maybe she loves that right now I'm wondering whether she's offering an olive branch or a kick in the stomach.

"Okay then," I tell her. "You love him. That's … great." I know I sound snotty, but really, what am I supposed to say?

She's still standing there, still looking at me. "And he loves me too."

Oh, no doubt. You don't offer a McDonald's employee a crash course on fruit-free parfait making for just *anyone.*

"You've only been dating a few months," I say.

"Almost a *year.*"

I squeeze the T-shirts between my fingers. "If you loved him, wouldn't you want the best for him?"

Olivia sets her jaw. "Of course I want the best for him."

I open my mouth to respond when we hear the bedroom door creak open.

"Ready to hit the beach?" Brian asks Bambi.

"Um ... " She tugs on her ponytail. "Give me a minute?"

He winks at her. "I'll be waiting."

He shuts the door and I scowl. Whether *I'm* ready to "hit the beach" or not is apparently a non-issue.

Olivia and I hold our gaze for a tense moment. That whole "I love him" thread—were we in the middle of that? Just getting started? Are we done now? Neither of us seems to know.

"Well," Olivia says, sounding resigned. "Guess I'll change into my bathing suit."

She plucks a tangerine-colored bikini from her suitcase and heads for the adjoining bathroom. I toss my T-shirts into a drawer, bite my lower lip, and bolt out of the room.

I follow the sound of Mom's vacuum cleaner into the great room. Without breaking my stride, I unclench my fist long enough to grab the cord of the vacuum cleaner and yank it from the outlet. Mom looks up, startled, as her vacuum cleaner abruptly shuts off.

"Why is she here?"

I can see Mom trying to settle into her cavalier oh-just-get-over-it-for-heaven's-sake mode, but I guess the steam emanating from my ears makes her think twice.

"Why. Is. She. Here?" I repeat.

"Shhh," Mom hisses, nodding toward my closed bedroom door just down the hall. "She'll hear you."

"*Tell me!* It is not fair that you sprung this on me!" I say, and, crazily, even in the midst of my rage, I'm wondering whether the word is "sprung" or "sprang." Dad's an editor; we think about these things.

Mom's knuckles blanch as she tightens her grip on the vacuum cleaner handle. "Not everything is about you, Forrest."

"Yeah? Well, *this* is. *I'm* the one stuck in a room with her."

"Oh, please. And will you keep your voice down!"

"Gladly. As soon as you answer the question: Why is she here?"

Mom tugs at her necklace. "Because I knew it would mean a lot to your brother."

"*Duh*. Except I thought we both agreed that what Brian *wants* these days isn't necessarily Brian *needs*."

She looks at me evenly. "Maybe that isn't for us to decide," she says in a clipped voice.

I fling my hands in the air. "Since when?"

"Since ... "

Mom and I both glance toward the hall as we hear doors open—first the one from my bedroom, then the one from Brian's. He and Olivia both emerge. Brian nods toward the beach. "Heading down," he says.

Mom nods. "We'll join you soon."

Brian and Olivia clasp hands and head out the back door, where Dad is doing a crossword puzzle on the deck.

Mom points to the electrical outlet, my cue that our conversation is over. Her vacuuming has been delayed as long as she can tolerate.

Whatever.

I plug it back in, give Mom a withering look as the vrooming resumes, and join Dad on the deck.

"Hi, Woodpecker," he says without looking up from his puzzle. I offer a sulky peace sign.

"Garrulous," Dad says.

"Too easy," I reply. "Plus, I'm not feeling very garrulous right now."

I plop in a deck chair next to his and peer at the ocean. "What was Mom thinking inviting her here?" I say, mostly to myself since Dad is generally on a need-to-know basis as far as Mom's affairs are concerned.

"It's a good sign," Dad says, still not looking up from his puzzle. "She's adjusting."

I eye him suspiciously. "Adjusting to what?"

He shrugs. "To letting you guys live your own lives. That'll come in handy for you too, you know. Wimp, eleven letters, first letter *M*."

"Milquetoast," I respond.

Dad jots it down. "Impressive," he murmurs under his breath. "I was assuming it would be some hip new colloquialism."

"'Hip,'" I repeat dryly. "Gee, Dad, you're so with it." I plant my chin in the palm of my hand. "She's a total flake, you know," I say, watching Brian and Olivia as they start splashing in the surf. "Just like her mom. You know her mom's not in the picture, right? She split when Olivia was, like, two. 'Split.' That's one of those hip new colloquialisms."

I expect Dad to chuckle, but instead he tosses me a Significant Look. "Don't judge people by their parents," he says.

I turn to face him. "Geez. What's up with *you*?"

"I mean it, Forrest," he says. Uh-oh. My real name. I really struck a nerve.

"It's true," I say. "About her mother, I mean."

"Even more reason to admire Olivia," he says.

My jaw drops. "Even *more*? Like we're tallying reasons to admire her? Hmmm: One, she looks smokin' hot in a bikini. Two, she looks smokin' hot in a bikini despite the fact that her mother ditched her when she was two."

Dad raises an eyebrow. "Enough."

I huff. It's extremely difficult to piss Dad off. Leave it to Olivia to provoke this response. One more reason to admire her, right?

But I forge ahead anyway. "Why don't we tally reasons *not* to admire her?" I say. "Like how she's totally unsuited for Brian and how she derailed his lifelong dream of medical school. And how I'm stuck sharing a room with her for a month."

"Be nice," Dad says, but his tone is lighter. He's doing his crossword puzzle again.

This emboldens me. "Why is everyone suddenly okay with Brian blowing off Vanderbilt?"

Dad fills in a word. "He's a big boy. He's entitled to live his own life." He tosses me a glance. "Just like you are."

"But I'm making *good* choices!"

Dad nods. "Good for you. Mom and I are proud of you. We really are. And we're proud of Brian—whatever his choices and however his life unfolds."

I turn my gaze back to the ocean, a sea breeze blowing through my hair. I shake my head slowly. "Just when I'm ready to stomp some sense into my stupid brother, you and Mom go all kumbaya on me."

Dad lays his puzzle aside, stands up, and tousles my hair. "How about stomping in the sand instead? Your mom will be out here soon with her cleaning supplies, and I'm not in the mood for a face full of Windex. Ready to hit the beach?"

I frown, but then scrunch my nose at him. "I'll grab the surfboards."

nine

"Wipeout!"

I point at Dad and laugh as his head bobs out of the water after being swamped by a wave. He gives me a thumbs-up sign and grabs his surfboard, unbowed and ready for another round.

I sit on my surfboard and use my arms to paddle deeper into the surf, the *whoosh* of the undertow skimming my legs. Spittles of seawater splash my face with every motion.

Once positioned waist-deep in the water, I face the beach, steady my surfboard, and wait. I let a few waves pass by. A better one is coming, and I'm patient. I can sense the biggest waves building, feel it deep in my bones. An eerie calm settles in, as if the sea is taking a deep breath in preparation for a convulsive heave.

"This is the one," I say to myself, then hop aboard the smoothly waxed fiberglass. I plant my feet firmly, slightly angled, then bend my knees and spread my arms, tipping left, then right, then left again, keeping myself balanced as the crest of the wave pushes me higher, higher, higher...

Then comes the adrenaline rush, riding the wave, owning the wave, as it blasts me to the shore in a mad, dizzying surge of pure energy.

I love how unpredictable the rides can be. Sometimes the *whoosh* subsides gradually, allowing me to teeter above the sea virtually until I reach the sand. Other times, the wild ride ends in a dizzying explosion in the water, me grasping my board desperately as the churning sea tosses me about and spits me out. No matter which way it shakes out—easy or hard—Dad and I invariably have grins on our faces as we get back on our feet.

It's supposed to be Dad and *Brian* and me riding the waves, of course. But Brian is lounging on a beach chair on the shore next to Olivia, their fingers lazily intertwined. This may be the first time I've ever seen Brian just *lie* on the beach. He's usually surfing, or jogging, or swimming, or throwing a Frisbee, or at least *reading*, for god's sake. But now he's lying there doing nothing. Such is life with Olivia.

I grab my board and walk toward them, shaking water from my ear.

"Wanna ride?" I ask Olivia, and okay, maybe just a touch of sadism is involved since I can only imagine how spastic she must look on a surfboard.

She peers up at me, shielding her eyes from the sun even though she's wearing sunglasses. "No thanks."

"Aw, c'mon. It's fun."

"She said no thanks," Brian mutters.

I curl my lip. "Thanks for the translation."

Olivia sits up straighter in her chair. "Really, thanks for the thought," she says. "I'm just not really up for it right now. My stomach's a little queasy."

I glance suspiciously at the half-eaten bag of chips by her side. Time to lurch for the nearest bathroom? I settle into a chair next to hers. If she really is bulimic, I want a ringside seat for verification. Maybe an eating disorder would be enough to nip Mom and Dad's sudden lovefest in the bud.

"So you're not the outdoorsy type," I say to Olivia.

I feel her eyes settle on me. "I didn't say that. I said my stomach was a little queasy."

Touché.

Dad calls Brian over for a game of Frisbee in the surf. Brian looks conflicted, but apparently another wordless conversation with Olivia's eyes convinces him it's okay to leave her in my evil clutches.

He squeezes her hand and trots off to join Dad.

"Hey, mind if I ask you something?" Olivia asks me.

Ummm...

"Shoot."

"Why don't you ever have any boyfriends?"

I literally gulp. What the hell...

"No offense," Olivia says earnestly, and have you ever noticed that the only times people say "no offense" are after they've offended you?

I feel blood pounding in my ears. How stupid that I'm speechless. What exactly do I feel? Indignation? Embarrassment? *I'm* the one who's supposed to knock Olivia off balance, not the other way around.

"I know you're only sixteen and all, but, I mean, look at you," Olivia says, eyeing my Speedo racerback. Frankly, I'm so flabbergasted at this point that I have absolutely no idea how to interpret that remark. Look at how hideous I am?

"You're gorgeous," Olivia says.

Oh. I didn't see that one coming.

"Right," I say, staring at my fingers as I twist them into pretzels.

"You *are*," Olivia says, and she seems too genuinely incredulous at the observation to sound like she's sucking up. "Your figure is amazing. And those green eyes and dimples? *Man.* Lots of guys in school talk about how cute you are, you know."

OMG, this is almost too revolting to bear.

"They *do*," Olivia continues. "I hear them. Or *over*hear them. You're a knockout."

I swallow hard, suddenly, ridiculously, on the verge of tears.

"But it's like you put out these vibes," Olivia says. She leans toward me. "Are you gay?"

Something about her casual guilelessness catches me off guard, and I answer the question as easily as she asked it: "No."

She nods. "I didn't think so. So what's up? Do you *want* to date?"

What kind of stupid, insane conversation *is* this?

"Forrest? Are you crying?"

I blink hard. "No. The sun's in my eyes."

Olivia takes off her sunglasses and locks eyes with mine. "I'm sorry. I didn't mean to..."

"I'm *fine*," I snap. "No, maybe I *don't* want to date. None of the guys in *our* town, anyway. Talk about a bunch of morons..."

Olivia nods, too eagerly. "Yeah, that's kind of what I thought... that you're too smart for the guys back home."

I blush. It's one thing for *me* to believe that; it's another for people to *believe* I believe that. I feel ridiculously exposed, excruciatingly pegged, revoltingly transparent.

"I give off vibes?" I ask in a small voice.

Olivia smiles. "Cool vibes," she assures me. "But kinda... intimidating."

I press a fingernail against my lower lip. "*I'm* the one who's intimidated," I say.

"What do you mean?"

I'm tempted to let the answer gush out as effortlessly as the rest of my true confessions: *I felt kinda pretty when I started high school, and I thought being popular was in reach. I mean, Brian is off-the-charts popular, right? But somehow, I can't pull it off, and the harder I try, the more of a laughingstock I make of myself. I'm too... what? Smart? Fashion-challenged? Nonconformist? I don't know, but I know I can't put my ego through the blender another time. Throw in a few goddesses like you who suck up all the attention, and—oh, and by the way, you're, like, my number-one disser. Besides, how superficial a goal is "popular"? And who needs those clowns anyhow?*

"I don't know ... " I say instead.

An awkward moment hangs in the air. "Well ... " Olivia finally says. "I think you're really pretty. I just wanted you to know."

Another awkward moment. I'm trying to stammer a response, but nothing comes out.

Olivia puts her sunglasses back on and settles back into her chair.

Thank you.

That's what I was going for.

ten

"How do you like your burgers, Oh-live-and-let-die?"

Olivia recoils. "I'm not really hungry."

I'm not sure which is more irritating: Olivia dissing Dad's burgers or Dad giving her nicknames (and McCartney-esque ones at that; sacrilege!).

"Ya gotta eat!" Dad says cheerily.

"Um ... maybe just a small one. And well done, please," Olivia says.

Okay, the spell has definitely been broken. Whatever cachet she accumulated earlier in the day with her "you're really pretty" comment has been obliterated by her "I'm a princess who can't eat my hosts' disgusting food" routine. What *is* it with this girl? Who doesn't eat *burgers*?

"How about if I make you a salad?" Brian cajoles into her ear.

"I *made* a salad," Mom snaps.

"Did you remember not to add any onions?" Brian asks, and OMG why don't we just hire a personal chef already for this insufferable diva.

"No onions," Mom says in a tight voice.

"I hate to be so much trouble," Olivia says, and then Dad starts chortling about how she's no trouble, no trouble at all, why, come to think of it, he's not a big fan of onions himself. Puh-leeze.

"And we have rolls, right, Mom?" Brian says. "Olivia really likes rolls."

"Who has rolls with hamburgers?" Mom asks sensibly, and I suppress a smile. What a weird development, that Mom is emerging as my beach BFF.

Olivia casts Brian an annoyed glance and he says, "Don't you like rolls?" And, god knows, we're all waiting with bated breath to hear the answer to this fascinating question.

She mouths a response to him that I can't decipher. It's quite the quandary to not be clear on her feelings regarding rolls.

I dig my fingertips into the arms of my cedar chair. Let's see: six five-day forecasts equals, hmmm, OMG, *ninety* meals, give or take a couple, and I'm not sure how much more of this I can stand.

"What *do* you like, Olivia?" I ask. "I mean, besides canta-loupe." *Oh, and celery. Remember the delicious celery we served at Brian's graduation party?*

She blushes. "I just don't have much of an appetite lately."

Brian glares at me. Really? *Really?* I'm having to suffer

through a game of Twenty Questions regarding her food preferences and *he's* glaring at *me*?

I suck in my lips and wonder if I'll end up hating Brian ninety meals from now. But as pissed as I am, I already know the answer to that. Nothing could make me hate Brian.

Not even Oh-live-and-let-diet.

———

"Ready for another?"

We've all watched in awe as Olivia wolfed down her well-done burger in two bites flat. So she's not made of porcelain after all.

"Um ... if you have enough," Olivia tells Dad. "I guess I was hungrier than I thought. That was delicious."

Brian smiles broadly. Mom, sitting safely in Olivia's periphery, rolls her eyes.

Dad heads back to the grill. "Another well-done burger coming up," he says.

"Um ... on second thought ... "

All eyes fall on Olivia, whose face has suddenly turned gray. She jumps up and runs into the house. Mom and Dad exchange glances, and Brian runs after Olivia.

"What the hell ... " I say, craning my neck to follow her path.

"Forrest," Mom sniffs. "Language."

"Do you think she's okay?" Dad asks Mom.

I jump to my feet. "No! It's not okay to puke after every meal!"

I glance at Mom, then Dad, then Mom again, but I can't read their expressions. Is bulimia one of those "hip new" diseases they can't wrap their heads around? Are we still in protect-Brian's-feelings-at-any-cost mode?

I squeeze my eyes shut, toss my paper plate aside, and stomp down the steps toward the beach.

———————

"It's a crab."

I furrow my brow.

"A horseshoe crab. Big whoop. People around here act like anything that washes up on the beach has fallen from Mars or something."

I look closer at the guy talking to me, then at the crowd of people he's referencing. And he's right: at least a dozen people are huddled around a spot a few yards up the beach peering down at the sand. I'm headed toward the crowd (not because I care what they're looking at but because I'm still trying to walk off my adrenaline overload), and the guy is headed toward me.

"A crab on the beach, huh?" I say. "Alert the media."

He chuckles. "You're headed in the wrong direction," he says. "You'll miss the sunset."

I hesitate.

"You need to walk *this* way," he persists, nodding his head west. "With *me.*"

His dark eyes sparkle as he smiles mischievously.

Whoa. Is he hitting on me?

He extends a hand and says, "I'm Scott."

I eye him warily for a moment, then shake his hand loosely. "Forrest."

His eyes widen. "Forrest?"

I nod. "Like the trees."

"I like trees," Scott says, then stoops slightly until his eyes are level with mine. "And I like sunsets even better. Join me?"

He's less cocky this time—maybe even a little nervous?—so after deliberating for a second, I nod.

"I can't go far," I say. "I, um, promised my mom I'd be home in time to do the laundry."

Okay, that sounded ridiculously lame. Why in the world did I feel the sudden need to create an impromptu escape hatch? *You're not a kid anymore, Forrest. Relax!*

Scott and I start walking, and before long we've matched each other's stride.

"Home, huh?" he says, the sea breeze tousling his sandy-blond hair. "You live here?"

"We have a beach house here," I say, and I catch myself as I almost point at it. It's embarrassing to tally how little experience I've had being flirted with, and god, he's cute. I need to be careful.

"Lucky," he says. "I'm staying at my aunt's place."

"Mmmmm."

"First day?" he asks.

"At the beach? Yeah. How'd you know?"

He grins. "Think I wouldn't have noticed you by now if you'd been here a while?"

I tug a lock of hair.

"You're blushing," Scott says.

"Am not."

"Are too."

I duck my head and smile. Geez. I guess I know how to flirt after all.

"So," Scott says, clapping his hands together. "Have you had a good first day?"

I shrug. "My brother's girlfriend is here. She's driving me a little crazy."

"The blonde?"

I look at him, startled.

"I saw the two of you on the beach earlier," he says.

My stomach tightens, but I tell myself to chill. *Flirting, meet Forrest. Forrest, meet Flirting.*

"She looks pretty high-maintenance," Scott says.

I laugh lightly. "Yeah. We've had in-depth discussions about her food preferences. So far, nothing is quite to her liking. Tragic, really. But I'm sure we'll hit on something she likes eventually. Only ninety more meals to go, give or take a couple."

Scott kicks the surf lazily with his heel. "So you'll be here a month?"

A wave washes over my feet. "Right."

"Yeah? Me too." He winks at me. "Thirty more sunsets to go, give or take a couple. They'll be a lot more beautiful if I have somebody to share them with. Besides my aunt, that is."

I bite my lip. Is this another setup, like Jake Bennett chatting me up a couple of weeks ago just to suss out information about Olivia?

"I'm sure you have plenty of people to share sunsets with," I venture cautiously.

"Maybe. But who do I *want* to share my sunsets with? That's the question."

Another trick question? I honestly don't know. So I ask him. "Who?"

He stops in his tracks, loosely takes my hands, and looks into my eyes. "You." His face inches closer. "I would give my right arm to share thirty sunsets with you."

Heat emanates from the back of my neck. "You don't even know me."

He lets my right hand drop, then brushes my nose with his index finger. "We can solve that problem." Pause. "I guess the question is ... do you *want* to solve that problem?"

Smile, Forrest, smile.

I smile but squeeze my arms together, suddenly a little chilled.

"Oooohh," Scott purrs. "*That* answers my question. You've got, like, the sexiest smile I've ever seen. Those are some serious dimples you've got going on. My dilemma is, do I gaze into that beautiful face? Or move on down south to your amazing body? You're making me crazy, Forrest-like-the-trees. Too much beauty to take in all at once. Yup. Thirty sunsets. I'll need at *least* that much time to worship your hotness."

Move on down south? I shift my weight nervously. Kind of an odd thing to say, but I'm silly to pick his words apart... right? I mean, this is how guys talk to girls... right? At least the smooth guys, the experienced guys, the guys who aren't immature morons like the ones at Peachfield High School... right? And, yeah, he's coming on pretty strong, but that's what guys do when they finally grow up enough to get their act together... right? It's cool when guys are confident enough to say what they mean. No stupid game playing.

Olivia's words from earlier in the day echo in my head: *Why don't you ever have any boyfriends?*

I swallow hard, then relax my shoulders.

Maybe it's time to start.

eleven

Shut. Keep them shut.

My strategy is to interact with Olivia as minimally as possible this month, and so, to set the tone on our first night together as roomies, I feign sleep when I hear her get out of her bottom bunk to make a bathroom run, even though I just came to bed a couple of minutes earlier.

It's easy to keep my eyes shut. The better to relive Sunset Number One with Scott. Sunset Number One. What a sap I've turned into in just the past few hours.

Not that anything really happened. He and I just walked for half a mile or so, the peach and mango colors of Sunset Number One streaking horizontally in the sky. Seems like we talked forever... though come to think of it, I still know next to nothing about him, like how old he is or where he's from. Oh well. We have twenty-nine more sunsets to cover all our bases.

Cover all our bases. I smile at the memory of Scott talking about "covering all the bases" with me, that silly adolescent guy talk, only he made it sound kinda…I dunno…adorable. And he didn't try anything; he was a perfect gentleman. He reached down and held my hand for a while, but it was so casual that it was clear he was just living in the moment. And, yeah, at one point, his arm slipped around my waist and his fingers started getting a little—how do I describe it—*adventuresome*, but hey, this is what guys do, right?

And he's so incredibly sweet that I know he would die if he thought he was making me uncomfortable, so all I'd have to do is give the word and his fingers would scurry away from my nether regions, and he'd probably be grinning that shy, amazing grin and telling me how sorry he was, that he didn't even realize where his hand was heading, that he was just so comfortable around me it was hard not to totally relax and be himself, but thanks for pointing it out, and he'd be much more careful from now on…

Anyway, that's about the time that I told him I needed to head back, and as soon as we turned around, I saw my parents in the distance, hand in hand farther up the beach. I told Scott I'd introduce him, but he said he just remembered he was scheduled to meet up with some friends and was probably already keeping them waiting, so he had to take off. He kissed my cheek at the last minute and reminded me I owed him twenty-nine more sunsets, then started jogging away from the surf.

I hear Olivia barf in the bathroom.

Okay, this is ridiculous.

So much for feigning sleep. When she emerges from the bathroom, I'm leaning up on an elbow. Her face looks chalky in the moonlight. She catches my eye and sucks in her breath slightly.

"You asked me a personal question earlier today," I say. "Now, can I ask you one?"

She swallows hard, then nods, tugging at her nightgown self-consciously.

"Are you bulimic?"

Olivia's eyes widen. "What?"

I climb down from my bunk and sit on the edge of her bed, staring at her squarely. "Barfing after every meal? What else can I think?"

Olivia's eyes narrow. "How about the truth? That I'm pregnant."

Oh my god.

My jaw drops.

"Pregnant..."

"I thought you knew," Olivia says.

"You're pregnant." I'm saying it more to myself than to her.

She sighs and sits next to me on her bed. "I didn't mean to shock you," she says. "I really thought you knew."

"Pregnant..." I clutch my chest. "Does Brian know?"

Olivia laughs. "Uh, duh."

I try to absorb the message, but my mind is already vaulting ahead. "My parents..." I mumble.

"They've known for two weeks," she says. "That's why I thought you knew."

Omigod. Omigod. Omigod.

Olivia puts a cool hand on my arm. "Breathe, Forrest. You look like you're about to hyperventilate."

"What ... what ... what are you gonna do?"

She smiles. "I'm gonna be a mom."

Jesus *Christ*!

I face her, then grab her arms. "Olivia, you've got to think this through. You're so young. Brian ... *he's* so young. He doesn't even have a real job. He needs to go to college. He needs to ... "

Olivia's eyes turn steely. "I know it'll take a while to get used to this," she says stiffly. "But Brian and I are going to be a family. Brian and our *baby* and I are going to be a family."

Yeah, that's a lovely sentiment, but since that's not possible ...

"What does my mom say about this?" I ask, and, I know, like, how desperate am I to invoke my *mother's* authority?

Olivia holds her frosty gaze for a moment, but then her face shrivels. She drops her head into her hands and sobs quietly. Her shoulders heave.

"Olivia ... I'm sorry ... I didn't mean ... "

I pat her clumsily.

"Olivia ... it's okay ... really ... "

She weeps a while longer, then looks up at me with tear-stained eyes and a quivery chin. "I guess you all think I'm a slut."

Yes.

"No. Nobody thinks that."

"I'm *not*," she says, her eyes crinkling again with a fresh set of tears. "I love Brian. I want to spend the rest of my life with him."

"But ... but ... how can you make it happen? You're so young ... "

"I'm eighteen," Olivia protests. "My mother had me at eighteen."

And we know how well that worked out.

I swallow hard. "So you're getting married?"

She nods and a smile seeps through the tears. "Will you be my maid of honor?"

Me in taffeta.

This day just keeps getting weirder by the second.

Brian and I are bobbing in the surf, splashing each other playfully in waist-high water. We're—I dunno—maybe seven and nine. In real life, Mom or Dad would definitely be hovering nearby at that stage in our lives, probably within arm's length of us, but in my dream, no adult is in sight. That's why I get a little nervous as I realize Bri keeps drifting deeper and deeper into the ocean.

At first, I keep my mouth shut—I pride myself on being a cool, unannoying little sister—but then it occurs to me that he doesn't realize he's drifting. He's chest-deep soon, then shoulder-deep, and now his chin is in the water, the waves threatening to swamp him altogether.

"You're too far out," I call, trying to sound casual.

But he's drifting even farther now. He's still smiling at me, still carefree, oblivious to the danger even as the waves start to wash over his head. "Too far!" I shout, urgently this time.

He cups a hand over his ear, his head now barely visible between waves. "What?"

He's so far from me now that I can hardly hear him. "Too far! Too far! Come back, Brian!"

But instead of swimming toward the shore, he gives me a thumbs-up. "I'm good!"

"No! You're too deep! You're too deep! I won't be able to save you!"

Now he's completely underwater, except for the thumb jauntily hoisted in midair.

"Too deep! Too deep!" I cry, now sobbing uncontrollably.

But he can't even hear me. He's drowning but still giving me a thumbs-up.

And there's nothing I can do to help him.

———————

I awake with a start, audibly gasping and feeling my heart pound against my chest.

God. What is it with these nightmares? If I keep this up, I'll fling myself off the top bunk before long.

Then I hear the steady rhythm of Olivia's breath as she sleeps in the bunk below. Moonlight seeps through the blinds, hazily illuminating the clock on the wall: 3:45 a.m. I hear waves sloshing lazily on the beach outside. My hands clench into fists as I realize that even though I'm wide awake now, I'm still stuck with the nightmare. Brian's life really *is* ruined. I really *can't* save him.

Too deep, Brian. Too deep...

———————

"How ya doing this morning, Evergreen?" Dad asks when I walk into the kitchen the next morning.

"Not pregnant."

Mom, Dad, and Brian cast furtive glances, their coffee mugs and orange juice glasses half empty on the kitchen table.

I pull up a chair and join them.

"So were you planning on telling me anytime within, say, the next nine months?"

Mom clears her throat. "We just found out ourselves," she says.

"*Two weeks ago*," I correct her. "God knows you've had time to nag me endlessly in the past two weeks. You couldn't have thrown in a quick 'Oh, by the way, Olivia is pregnant'?"

Brian shushes me and glances anxiously toward the family room.

"She's still fast asleep," I assure him. "Spending the whole night hurling tends to have that effect. And thanks for that, by the way. Another reason I'm nominating her for Roomie of the Year."

Brian's face darkens. "And you wonder why we didn't tell you."

I sigh. "I was kidding."

"No, you weren't," he mutters, tapping his fork against his plate.

"Guys," Dad says wearily. "We've got enough to deal with without the two of you going at it."

Tears suddenly spring into my eyes. "I can't do anything right with you anymore," I tell Brian.

Anger flashes in his eyes. "Be nice to the girl I love. That's it. That's all I ask."

I lean closer toward him. "She's changing your whole life!"

He nods smartly. "Yeah. And considering I think that's a good thing, isn't it about time that you butt out?"

I rub my eyes roughly with the heels of my hand. This is crazy. The last time I cried to Brian, he practically did back flips to cheer me up. I'd submitted an essay for a newspaper contest, and when I didn't win, my English teacher confided that one of the judges told him he thought it was "good ... *too* good, if you know what I mean," meaning I guess he thought it was plagiarized, which my English teacher assured him was total shit. But whatever, I still didn't win the contest, and when I cried like a baby that evening at the dinner table, Brian put an arm around me, pressing me against his side and fuming with indignation about the injustice of it all.

And now he's just glaring at me.

"Guys!" Dad beseeches. "We're a family. We pull *together* at times like these."

Brian shakes his head and laughs wryly. "'Times like these,'" he repeats, a bitter edge in his voice. "Exactly what kind of a *time* is it, Dad, other than the best time of my life?"

Mom squeezes her eyes together and slaps the table. "Will everyone *please eat their breakfast*!"

I glare at Brian. "Not hungry."

I get up and walk back to my bedroom. Olivia's still in bed, squeezing the sleep out of her eyes.

"Hi," I say. "Hey, Olivia, can I ask you a favor?"

She props up on her elbows. "Sure."

"Think I can borrow one of your bikinis today?"

twelve

I toss my book aside and look at Olivia, the waves just beginning to nip at our beach chairs as the tide comes in.

"Wanna walk?" I ask.

She smiles apologetically. "Maybe later? I'm still kinda queasy."

"No problem."

She adjusts her sunglasses and lays her magazine on her tanned stomach. "You look smokin' hot in my bikini, by the way," she tells me, and I blush.

"Thanks." I get up and head toward the surf.

How stupid was I to think Scott would just magically materialize by my beach chair this morning? He doesn't even know which house is mine, and come to think of it, I don't know which one is his. Maybe he'd walked two miles before our paths crossed. Maybe I'll never see him again.

And maybe it's just as well. He *was* pretty pushy, after all; he obviously knows his way around girls. But is that a bad thing? I mean, *I'm* the freak who sits at home on Saturday nights reading Faulkner. Besides, he was pushy in kind of an adorable way. I like how he wouldn't take no for an answer, that even though I was in my cutoffs and T-shirt, he was digging on me. Me! Of all the girls on the beach.

Why didn't I show him which house was mine? I had the chance and I blew it. Was I expecting him to consult his crystal ball to find me? *Stupid, stupid, stupid!*

Well, one thing's for sure: the longer I sit in my beach chair, the slimmer the odds of our sharing Sunset Number Two. Or three... or four...

I tug at my bikini bottom (who can be comfortable in something the size of a washcloth?) and walk down the beach, trying to look nonchalant. I actually *do* get a couple of second glances—more than a couple, really—and I think maybe I can get the hang of being a goddess.

I scan the beach every so often, then check out the swimmers, looking for that mop of sandy-blond hair. Shelley would never believe this: me actually pursuing a guy.

But I'm not really pursuing him, right? *He's* the one who penciled me in for the next twenty-nine sunsets. And besides, all I'm doing is taking a walk on the beach, which is probably what I'd be doing if I'd never met him, and geez, it's a free country, isn't it, and...

Oh god. There he is. He's playing Frisbee with three other guys just a few yards up the beach. He's even cuter than I remembered, tanned and shirtless with khaki shorts that ride low and loose on his hips. I mean, not *ridiculously* low and loose, not like he's about to star in a Flo Rida video or anything, just like he never really considers throwing on anything other than his comfiest clothes, and they just happen to fit him low and loose, but snug enough to stay put when he lunges for a Frisbee, like he's doing now, and...

My heart is about to beat through my chest (you can't tell that by looking, right, even if you're wearing a bikini?) but a play-it-cool mantra is doing a forced march through my brain. I'm so insanely happy to see him that I almost trot right over (wouldn't it be cool and adorable if I swooped in just in time to catch the Frisbee he's lunging for?), but I don't want to make an ass of myself, so I just keep walking, peering mysteriously into the distance.

As I get closer, I wait for him to call out my name (*Hey, Forrest-like-the-trees!*), but he's pretty preoccupied with his game. The guys are all laughing and whooping, high-fiving and diving into the sand. Yeah... this is better: he hasn't even noticed me yet, and I'm too intrigued by whatever I'm peering at in the distance to notice him, so it won't be until just after I pass him that my turquoise bikini catches his eye. Then he'll think, *Wow, what a smokin' hot girl,* and then he'll do a double-take and realize, *OMG, that's Forrest!* and he'll trot up and grab my arm, and I'll register just a hint of faux-confusion in my eyes before I look closer and realize, *OMG, that's Scott!* and we'll laugh and plan to spend our second sunset together, with maybe dinner thrown in this time for good measure.

So I just keep walking, head jauntily high and shoulders straight, my arms swinging lazily.

But I've walked past him now, and...nothing. He and his friends are still laughing and whooping, consumed with their game, oblivious to me.

Chill, Forrest, chill.

Right. So what. I'm just taking a walk on the beach, right? Really, it's pretty clear by my mysterious expression that I actually *prefer* to be left alone, to keep myself company with my own profound thoughts. Uh-oh—is that the intimidation factor Olivia was talking about? I'm not sure; in the past, I really *haven't* given a crap. No play-it-cool pep talks needed. Has my mantra made me more intimidating than ever, too intimidating to approach?

I don't think so. From the sound of their horseplay, they really do seem clueless.

Scott just didn't notice me, that's all. My pulse quickens. I can't make the same mistake I made last night, counting on fate to throw us back together. I've got to put myself out there. I've got to get in the game.

I turn around, face the guys, put my pinkies in the sides of my mouth, and whistle.

Two of the guys look at me, but not Scott. The third guy follows the gaze of the first two, so now three of them are looking at me. But still not Scott. So I wave my arms over my head.

"Hey, stranger!"

Yes. I really say that. I'm whistling, waving my arms over my head, and yelling lame things. *Why not just erect a billboard, Forrest?*

But it's okay, right? I mean, it's cute. Guys are flattered by attention, especially when their friends are around. So, yes, I'm about as subtle as an air traffic controller, but that's better than being intimidating.

But Scott *still* isn't looking at me. One of his friends jostles him and points in my direction. Scott looks at me, registers a hint of something I can't quite put my finger on (annoyance?), then immediately looks away again. He claps his hands a couple of times to signal the others to resume the game.

What the hell...?

I'm still standing there, frozen in my spot. He must not recognize me. Understandable, right? I mean, last night I was wearing a baggy T-shirt.

"It's me," I call. "Forrest."

Scott glances at me again for a nanosecond, tosses the slightest of waves, and lunges for the Frisbee.

Oh. He *does* recognize me. He recognized me all along, including when I was making a total fool of myself by making like a windmill. He might have even noticed me earlier, as I was approaching him. The upshot is clear: he knows who I am. He just doesn't care.

But how can that be? He's the one who friggin' hit on me! When I was wearing a baggy T-shirt, for crying out loud! I put on a bikini for this jerk!

My cheeks are so hot, my heartbeat so ferocious, that I wonder if I'll hyperventilate right there on the beach, and wouldn't *that* be the cherry on top of my goddess sundae. Maybe I should go vomit on his feet. I could write a book at this point about how to repel a guy.

Move, Forrest, move.

Right. Standing in this spot like a statue is really not working for me. Time to move on. But do I turn around and head back for my beach chair?

Of course not! That'll make it obvious that the only point of my beach walk was to stalk Scott. I've got to keep pushing forward.

So I do. I trudge along the surf, white-hot heat emanating from my cheeks, wondering how on earth I could have deluded myself *again* into thinking I was something I'm clearly not.

I walk a long, long way, fueled by the adrenaline rush of humiliation and determined not to cross Scott's path again. After an hour or so, I feel my nose and shoulders tingle from sunburn. Good. Maybe I'll spontaneously combust. Brian hates me, Scott hates me, and god knows I hate myself in this stupid what-the-hell-were-you-thinking turquoise bikini.

What a self-deluded fraud I am. What a loser.

I guess it's time to turn around. I've got to head back sometime.

But first, I fall into the surf and splash my face with water.

Now nobody will notice my tears.

thirteen

It's 3:40 a.m.

I do a quick calculation on my fingers, then tell Olivia as she tiptoes back to bed in the dark, "Five hours."

"What?"

"You've gone five hours tonight between barfing. That's the best you've done all week."

She giggles lightly, the springs in her bottom bunk squeaking as she settles in. "Sorry," she says. "I didn't know I've been waking you up."

"It's okay," I tell her, the moonlight seeping through the window like a gauzy warm blanket. "What's it like to be sick all the time?"

Olivia laughs ruefully. "My doctor says pregnancy isn't a state of sickness, it's a state of health. I think he's in a state of denial."

I smile. Olivia had a reputation in high school as a total airhead, and, granted, I don't think she'll be delving into quantum physics anytime soon, but she's brighter than I gave her credit for.

"Seriously," I say. "Doesn't it get you down having to sprint to the bathroom twenty times a day?"

Olivia pauses, then replies, "I don't mind. It's a reminder that even though he's the size of a jelly bean now, he's right here, safe and sound."

My brow furrows. "You already know it's a boy?"

"No," Olivia says sleepily. "It's way too early for that. But it feels like a boy to me ... I guess because he seems so much like Brian."

"So Brian makes you barf twenty times a day?"

Olivia laughs again. "Well, indirectly, yes." She sighs. "I just love my baby so much. I guess that's why he seems like Brian."

I knit my fingers together. Yes, I'm getting used to the fact that she's pregnant, but I'm not getting used to this sense of inevitability. As in *Duh, of course Brian and Olivia are going to have a baby. Of course they'll be a family. Of course Brian's future is set in stone.*

I'm thinking we're in an all-of-our-options-are-still-on-the-table kind of phase. Not that I get a vote, of course, and not that I even know what that means. I can't think too hard about the specifics: how I feel about abortion in general, how I'd feel about my own niece or nephew being aborted, how I'd feel about my niece or nephew being somewhere out in the world with a different family...

I shudder.

Okay, *now* I'm thinking about it. And it sucks.

But still... Brian being body-slammed into a precarious-at-best future at the age of eighteen? That makes me shudder too. Then again, Brian sure isn't *acting* like he's being body-slammed. He's acting like he's voluntarily thrown himself at Olivia's feet, and there's nowhere he'd rather be.

"Speaking of being down..." Olivia says hesitantly, and my brain does a quick replay for a reference point.

"What?" I prod her.

"You've seemed... down lately."

I swallow. I've been trying really hard the past few days to cut the crap with Olivia. Really, I have. Yes, the pregnancy revelation totally freaked me out at first, but hey, it is what it is, and whatever the future holds, Olivia and I are bonded for life at this point. I mean, she's carrying my DNA around in her uterus. Even if that disappears tomorrow—through whatever mechanism it might disappear, which I'm now consciously willing myself not to think about—we're connected now in a cosmic kind of way. I don't know how I feel about that. I just know I feel it.

And frankly, the pregnancy makes her interactions with Brian considerably less puke-inducing than before. They're not a couple of lovestruck kids anymore contemplating the intricacies of fruit-free McDonald's parfaits. They're parents. God, that's hard to absorb.

Plus the fact that she notices way more than I ever gave her credit for. All those curled lips and narrowed eyes in high school? Maybe I was misinterpreting. Maybe she was trying to figure me out rather than judging me.

And who'd have thought she would notice the funk I've been in for the four days that have passed since Sunset Number One, which, *gasp*, shockingly turned out to be Sunset Number Finito?

My fingers are still looping in and out of knots. I take a deep breath. "I met a guy."

Pause.

"Really?"

I shake my head, grateful Olivia can't see me blush. "It's nothing. *Truly* nothing. It's so stupid. I just…I met this guy on the beach our first night here. We took a walk together. He kinda…indicated I'd be seeing more of him. And the crazy thing is, I really wanted to. Then I saw him on the beach the next day and he blew me off."

The sound of the surf lapping onto the shore sounds like a heartbeat.

"Oh," Olivia says.

Why did I tell her this? Was I concerned that she still wasn't quite clear on my status as a loser? Stupid, stupid, stupid.

"Hey, if he's not into you," Olivia says, aiming for breezy but conveying a mortifying hint of pity, "then who needs him. Move on."

"Right..."

"I mean it, Forrest. You're amazing. You're smart, and you're gorgeous, you're..."

Oh god, please make this stop.

"...drop-dead beautiful," Olivia continues, and my nails are piercing my palms so hard, they just might be drawing blood. "And you can do *sooooo* much better than some jerk who blows you off a day after—"

She stops abruptly, the wheels in her brain clearly spinning.

"A day after *nothing*," I assure her. "We didn't even kiss. It was just a stupid walk on the beach. I can't believe I'm making a deal about it. I can't believe I'm *talking* about it."

Maybe I can convince her in the morning that this conversation was just a dream. Maybe I can hitchhike to Mexico and start a new, humiliation-free life.

"I'm glad you told me," Olivia says, and hey, that makes one of us.

"I mean it," she says. "I never had anybody to talk to about this kind of thing."

I bend over the side of the bunk to look her in the eye. "*What* kind of thing? Guys have never done anything but worship the ground you walk on."

Olivia shakes her head. "Do you really believe that?"

"*Hello*, I've witnessed it," I say, then hop off my bunk and sit on the edge of her bed.

I sit there for a moment, then hear her sniffle.

"Olivia?"

She dabs her eyes.

"Olivia? Are you crying?"

She shakes her head roughly. "It's nothing, just hormones..."

"No way. Something's wrong. What is it?"

She sniffles some more. "I just... it's just nice to have somebody to talk to."

I pull a lock of hair behind my ear. "You have Brian."

She nods quickly. "I know, I know. He's great. But I mean a girl. I've never really had girlfriends."

My eyebrows knit together. "What about Casey and the other cheerleaders?"

Olivia shrugs. "They're not real friends. They're catty bitches, to be honest... a few of them, anyway. They hung around me because we were on the squad together, but everything was so competitive. They were always making little digs to knock me off balance. Maybe because my mom's not in the picture? I dunno... I've never been able to figure out why girls are always weird around me. Your friend, Shelley: that's a *real* friend. Good friends build you up, not knock you down."

I press in my lips. "It really pissed me off when you and Casey were dissing Shelley at the graduation party."

Olivia's eyes widen. "It was Casey, not me!"

I stare at her evenly, and she blushes.

"You're right," she says. "I should've spoken up. The way you stood up for Shelley? That was... incredible. I thought to myself that very instant, *That's the difference between Forrest and me.*"

I bite my lower lip. "I don't always stick up for people." I feel a stab in my stomach, thinking of the times I've either halfheartedly defended Olivia or snarkily dissed her myself.

She smiles. "I just envy that you have friends," she says. "And your mom."

My eyes narrow. "You've got a mom too. I met her, remember? At the football game? I thought she was your sister?"

I feel a pinch in my chest as I remember their laughter as I walked away, incredulous about what an idiot I was.

"She loved that," Olivia says in a small, tight voice. "She's probably told that story a million times: 'Olivia's friend thought I was her sister!'" Her face crinkles again.

"Isn't that a good thing?" I say consolingly, not sure if I should touch her or not. "I mean, isn't it cute that your mother is so gorgeous, people think you're sisters?"

More sniffles. I reach over to the dresser, pluck a tissue from the box, and hand it to Olivia.

"I wouldn't mind people thinking I had a sister if I had a mother," she says bitterly.

"But…you were laughing too. I remember."

Olivia's dewy eyes stare into space, a mixture of contempt and despair. "I want a *real* mom. Not some beauty queen who breezes into town a few times a year to try to outshine me."

Now I *do* touch her... tentatively at first, resting my hand on her arm, then squeezing gently. "Does she know you're pregnant?"

Olivia nods, still staring into space. "It just gives her more ammunition to tear into my dad. He's a moron, how could he let this happen, she saw it coming a mile away, blah, blah, blah, blah, blah. Oh, and the baby's supposed to call her Aunt Olivia. She doesn't want anybody knowing she's a grandmother."

The waves are still pumping their gentle heartbeat.

"Your mom's name is Olivia too?"

Her eyes narrow. "I hate it. I hate my stupid name." Then her gaze suddenly softens. "I've tried to get Brian to call me something different. I know it sounds stupid, but something like Liv—some people call me that—or even my initials, OJ..."

"Yeah, *that's* not gonna work," I wisecrack, and Olivia giggles.

"It doesn't matter," she says. "Brian says nothing sticks, and besides, he loves my name and he wants me to love it too. He says you have to love all of yourself, even the things you hate, before you can really open your heart to someone else."

I wrinkle my nose. "I think he read that on a Hallmark card," I tease, and I'm relieved when Olivia laughs.

"But he's right," she says wistfully. "If I hate my mom, or my name, or my thighs, or whatever ... that just sucks up energy that I should be using to love my life, to love the people in my life. Like my baby."

"Deep," I say, and I actually really mean it. How ridiculous does my guy-on-the-beach story sound now?

Olivia peers at me and says, "I'm sorry that guy on the beach hurt your feelings."

OMG. My skin actually tingles as I wonder if she just somehow read my mind.

"I'm thinking we should go bikini shopping and make him eat his heart out," she continues.

I shrug. "Embarrassingly enough, I actually sorta tried that. The day I borrowed your bikini? Didn't work. Besides, I'm more of a Speedo kind of girl."

But Olivia looks determined. "Bikini shopping. Tomorrow."

Whatever expression I have on my face makes her press harder. "Trust me," she says. "This is my area."

"I'm well aware that fabulosity is your area," I say, and again, I'm relieved when she laughs.

"You know what pisses me off the most?" I say. "I feel like he stole the beach from me. I haven't even been able to walk on the friggin' beach for fear of running into him."

"Oh, you'll do more than *walk* on the beach," Olivia says. "You're gonna *strut* on the beach. You're gonna *own* the friggin' beach."

Now she's making *me* laugh.

And as improbable as it seems, I'm thinking: Sure. Why not. What the hell.

Yes.

What the hell.

fourteen

"But I made pancakes!"

I glance at Olivia, who's turning gray just from the very mention of the word.

"Sorry, Mom," I respond, "but we want to get an early start."

Mom puts her fork on her plate, peering at me incredulously. "An early start on shopping? *You?*"

"Wacky, huh?" I say, sticking my head in the refrigerator. "Liv, want a cola for the road?"

"Cola!" Mom moans. "You girls need some food!"

"What are you shopping for?" Brian asks, setting his own fork aside.

Olivia shrugs as I hand her a Coke. "Just stuff."

She and I giggle, at which point a veritable flurry of alarmed glances unfolds at the breakfast table. I'm not sure what has them more flummoxed: my sudden BFF status with Liv (hey, she said she prefers it) or my newfound penchant for shopping.

"What kind of stuff?" Dad asks.

"Uzis, ammo, that kind of thing," I say, popping the lid of my can.

Olivia laughs some more. "She's kidding," she tells Brian. "We're buying bathing suits."

"*More* bathing suits?" Mom says, and it's obvious she's referring to Olivia's stash, not mine.

Olivia bristles a bit. "They're for Forrest."

"And, hey, I might even pick out a couple of baby outfits while I'm at it," I say.

Mom's face blanches as she casts a panicked glance at Dad.

"What?" I ask, looking from Mom to Dad, then back again.

"It's awfully early for that," Mom says, still looking at Dad. When Dad doesn't respond, her brow furrows.

"I think that's really nice, Forrest," Brian says, getting up from the table to put his dish in the sink.

"A compliment from my bro? I can die happy now."

He punches my arm playfully, then pecks Olivia on the cheek. "Want me to come?" he asks her.

She shakes her head without looking up.

"Not unless you need some new bikinis," I tell him.

"I'm good," he says.

Olivia and I walk into the family room and grab our purses, Mom's eyes boring into the back of my head.

"You girls have fun," Dad says, and I turn around in time to see Mom glaring at him.

I linger for just a second, wondering what's up with that. But then I hurry to catch up with Olivia, who's already rushing out the door.

She can't seem to get out of here fast enough.

———

"Is just the *thought* of me in a bikini making you sick to your stomach?"

Silence.

Olivia has been pale since we walked out the door. Now she's biting the nail of her pinkie, pitched nervously forward as she backs out of the driveway.

"Hello?" I say, waving my hands as she pulls into the street.

She glances at me. "Sorry. What did you say?"

"Are you about to hurl?" I ask her.

"No. Why?"

"You just look kinda ... are you okay?"

Olivia's eyes turn doleful. "Your mother hates me."

"Mom? No," I say unconvincingly.

"She's never liked me," Olivia says. "Then I spring the pregnancy on her, and ... "

"She really seems okay with it," I say, and this time, I mean it. I'd have guessed a full-scale meltdown, and instead, Mom seems eerily complacent. She didn't so much as utter a word about the pregnancy for two weeks, for crying out loud, at least not in front of me. I mean, I know she's not jumping for joy or anything, but she and Dad are apparently rolling with the punches. Of course, Dad always rolls with the punches.

"Did you see how she reacted when you mentioned baby clothes?" Olivia says, her fingernail still hovering by her mouth.

"Well, like she said, it's kinda early to be ... "

"I was so happy when she invited me on this beach trip," Olivia says, her voice breaking. "I thought, *Wow, I'm part of the family now*. I mean, I know the only reason she's accepting me is because of the baby, but still, if she wanted me along on your family trip, then she must think ... "

"Right," I say reassuringly. "You're part of the family. And kudos to you for thinking that's a good thing."

She doesn't laugh.

"Olivia," I say firmly. "You're family now."

She tosses me a grateful but unconvinced smile. We drive in silence for a couple of moments, then she says, "It wasn't my idea for Brian to blow off Vandy, you know. I tried to talk him into going."

I swallow hard.

She looks at me from the corner of her eye. "Is that why you hate me too? Hated me?"

My hands fumble in my lap. "Of course not. Brian is responsible for his choices, not you."

"But his choice would have been Vandy if it hadn't been for me. That's what you think?"

What do I say? Duh?

"He's been freaking out about college all year," Olivia says. "He felt so much pressure to make his mother proud, to go to Vandy, to be a doctor... it broke my heart to see him so stressed. The first few months we were dating, he was breaking out in rashes, like, every other week. It's only when he decided to stay home that he seemed like himself again. And he made that decision *before* I got pregnant, remember."

Yeah. I remember. And now that she mentions it, I remember the rashes too.

"But he *wanted* to go to medical school," I say.

"He wanted to please your mom. And there's nothing wrong with that. But, man, the guilt did such a number on him. It almost made me grateful I didn't *have* a mom."

I peer at her. "Has she ever been in your life?"

Olivia shrugs. "She shows up on our doorstep every few months to create drama for my dad. That's all she cares about: making his life miserable. She doesn't care anything about me."

I feel a stab in my heart to hear her sound so matter-of-fact.

I stare out the passenger window and watch a blur of fuchsia crepe myrtle. "Why did she leave?" I ask.

Olivia shrugs again. "A guy, I think. Or maybe a job. She was gonna be a model. I don't remember ever living with her." She laughs wryly. "Wouldn't you think that would mean I wouldn't miss her? I mean, if you grow up never remembering having your mom in your life, you shouldn't miss her, right? It should be like ice cream: the only way you can miss it is if you remember what it tastes like. If you don't remember, you don't know what you're missing. So you don't miss it."

"But...you miss *her*."

Olivia's expression darkens. "I hate her."

Wow. "You don't mean that."

"I totally do. So when your mom hugged me when I told her I was pregnant and said everything was gonna be okay, then invited me to your *beach* house, I..."

Her eyes fill with tears.

"Mom's gonna be fine," I tell her. "It's just...she can't go more than two weeks without filling her bitchy quota. It's probably best you found out sooner rather than later. It's the cross we all bear."

Olivia giggles through her tears. "I loved it when you called me Liv," she says.

I nod smartly. "Well, long Liv the queen. Just remember that Mom is the queen."

Her eyes sparkle. "Can I be the princess?"

"God, yes. I look like crap in a tiara."

———

"So, what's his name?"

I look up quizzically from the drink I'm sipping. "Whose name?"

Olivia dangles a fry outside her mouth. "The guy who's gonna eat his heart out when he sees you in your new bikini."

I blush. "Oh. I dunno. Who cares."

Olivia nods sharply as kids zoom around the periphery of the fast-food restaurant. "Exactly. Yes, we want him to eat his heart out, but you have *so* moved on. That's what lover boy needs to know. We need you walking on the beach holding hands with some hot new guy by sunset."

I laugh. "Yeah, hot guys and I go way back. I just snap my fingers and they magically appear."

"Oh, they'll appear all right," Olivia says. "Stick with me, girlfriend. We'll have 'em eating out of your hand."

I swallow a bite of my burger. "Hey, you've gone all morning without barfing," I note.

Olivia smiles. "Yeah. Maybe I'm turning the corner." She strums her fingers lazily on the plastic tabletop. "I had fun hanging out with you this morning."

"Yeah. Me too." I lean in a bit. "You know how you talked about Brian freaking out about college?"

She tilts her head. "Yeah?"

"I'm a little freaked out too. I can hardly stand the thought of eleventh grade, much less college."

Olivia's eyebrows widen. "Really? I thought you loved school. Aren't you, like, borderline genius or something?"

I blush. "Yeah, Einstein's got nothing on me. And that

whole 'genius' vibe does wonders for my social life, by the way."

"So weird," Olivia says, studying my face closer. "You seem so totally confident. I always thought you were, like, the ultimate cool chick."

I'm tempted to say something glib, but I think better of it. "I think the best way to hide your insecurity is to act like you don't give a shit."

Olivia bounces lightly in her seat. "It totally works!" she gushes, and I laugh at her earnestness.

"I mean it," she continues. "It just blows my mind that you're so ... *different* than I thought." She leans in for a sensitivity check. "I don't mean that as an insult at all, I really don't ... "

"No, I get it," I assure her. "I'm actually having to rethink some impressions of my own."

She points playfully at herself. "Diva?"

"Like, *duh*," I tease, and she laughs.

Then she wrinkles her nose. "Does everybody think that?" she asks warily.

"No, I think there are some Aborigines in Australia who haven't gotten the memo."

Her eyes sparkle. "You're, like, the funniest person I know."

"And you're the most diva-licious." I hoist my Coke toward her and she taps it with hers.

"I think we make a fabulous pair," she says.

And it's the damndest thing that I'm starting to think the same thing myself.

fifteen

I hear the front door slam as we pull into the driveway.

Brian bolts out the door, his face white-hot with rage. He's barefooted, so he can't be going far. I guess this occurs to him, because rather than continuing to bolt toward the driveway, he pivots and walks around the side of the house toward the beach.

Olivia and I exchange alarmed glances. "I'll go catch up with him," she says, and I nod. She gets out of the car and heads in his direction, her brisk walk morphing into a trot.

I grab the shopping bag from the back seat, get out of the car, and stand there a moment. Should I follow Brian too?

Of course not, moron.

Still, I'm dying to know what's up. I linger a moment longer, then head for the front door. I can hear shouting before I walk inside. Shouting? My parents never shout. What is *up*?

I gently creak open the door. Their shouts are coming from the deck. I can see them from the foyer, but they don't seem to notice me. I inch closer, straining to overhear.

"Quit trying to micromanage everything!" Dad is telling Mom. "You're just going to drive him away!"

"He's not going to ruin his life on my watch!" Mom responds, her hands flying in midair.

"He's not on your watch anymore, dammit. He's eighteen years old!"

"Eighteen!" Mom repeats. "Eighteen! Is this really what you want for him, Michael? To carve his future in stone at age eighteen? To shut off all of his options before he can even grasp what that means?"

"It doesn't matter what *we* want for him," Dad snaps. "It's *his life*, Maureen!"

Mom's eyes narrow. "Yeah, well, maybe you don't get a vote."

Stunned silence. Even from my vantage point, I can feel the jolt of electricity that Mom's words have sent coursing through the air.

"What the hell does that mean?" Dad asks in a steely voice.

Mom pauses. "I'm sorry," she finally says, sounding anything but. "But I mean it. This is one time I won't let you stand in my way. There's too much at stake."

"So I'm suddenly an outsider, huh?" Dad yells, and it's at that moment that Mom glances in my direction.

Her face turns white. Dad follows her gaze. We all seem

frozen in place. My brain replays the past few moments, trying to make sense of them. My normally prim mother shouting at the top of her lungs? My normally placid dad yelling back? Dad not getting a vote, being a sudden outsider? What the hell?

I finally jolt myself into motion, walking through the house and joining them on the deck. I cross my arms and face them.

"Forrest…" Mom says. "We didn't know you were…we were just…"

"We were just headed for the beach," Dad says softly.

"I don't think so," I say, glaring at them.

"Don't be ridiculous," Mom says. "We were just having a discussion that got a little heated, that's all. It was nothing."

"What's. Going. On."

Mom huffs. "This is nothing to make a federal case about, for heaven's sake. Dad and I had a spat. That's all."

Dad stuffs his hands in the pockets of his shorts, staring at the ground.

"You went two weeks without telling me Olivia was pregnant," I say. "*Two weeks*. And even then, *you* didn't tell me, *she* did. Now you're keeping more secrets …"

"*Keeping secrets*," Mom repeats, her voice dripping with ridicule. "We're your parents, Forrest, not the CIA."

"I'm a member of this family too!" I bellow. "Or do I not 'get a vote' either? What's up with that, Dad? Why don't you get a vote?"

He looks at me warily, then opens his mouth to speak.

"Oh, *for heaven's sake!*"

Mom's shrill voice makes both of us jump.

"I wanted to give Brian some advice," Mom continues, her hands flapping again. "Your father disagreed. I told him he didn't get a vote. I'm Brian's *mother*. Mothers have instincts that fathers don't have."

I'm still looking at Dad. His eyes fall.

"*End of discussion!*" Mom says, then walks inside, slamming the door behind her.

A breeze sets our wind chime in motion, a discordant jangle of tinny pings.

I keep staring at Dad until his eyes meet mine. "Tell me what's going on," I say.

"Your mom just told you," he says, but his eyes fall again.

"Bullshit."

"*Forrest.*"

"I mean it, Dad. I'm sorry, but you're obviously keeping something from me."

He studies his hands. "Kids don't necessarily need to know everything their parents know."

Dad is terrible at keeping secrets. If I wait him out, I sense he'll keep talking.

"What you need to know," he finally says, "is how much your mom and I love you and Brian. Unconditionally. With all of our hearts. Period."

I study him closely. "Except there's more to know," I say. The tinny wind chimes keep pinging in the breeze.

Dad opens his mouth, but Mom suddenly flings the door back open. "I told you both," she says, "*end of discussion.*"

I'm still staring Dad down, but the moment is lost. He walks over to me and kisses my forehead. "Let's drop it for now. Okay?"

Then he and Mom walk into the house, leaving the door ajar. I kick a deck chair with my tennis shoe, then walk down the steps toward the beach.

sixteen

Brian is sitting in the surf in his shorts, staring at the horizon. My eyes dart around for signs of Olivia. I don't see her.

I run to Brian and sit beside him, the waves lapping at our feet. I'm still wearing tennis shoes, but I don't care that they're getting wet. All I care about is the stricken look on my brother's face.

"Tell me what's going on," I say, leaning into his face.

He runs a hand through his dark curls and drops his head.

"What *is* it, Brian?"

"It's ... "

His voice breaks, and my heart crumbles into pieces.

"What's going on?" I repeat. "And where's Olivia?"

He points vaguely down the beach. "Walking. I tried to go with her, but she said she wanted to be alone for a while." He swallows hard. I put my hand on his back.

"I heard Mom and Dad yelling when we got back," I say. "Is it about the baby?"

He lifts his chin defiantly. "The only reason Mom invited Olivia to the beach was to try to talk her into giving the baby up for adoption."

My jaw drops.

"*My baby.*" He punches a fist into the palm of his hand. "She honestly thought I'd be willing to walk away from my baby."

"You must have misunderstood ... "

"She's already got a family lined up!" he says with mock gusto. "This great couple at our church! *Awesome* couple! Can't have kids of their own, so, hey, my baby actually comes in kinda handy. It's like it was meant to be! And if *that* falls through, maybe a yard sale ... ? You know ... buy our old lawn mower, and we'll throw in the baby for an extra two bucks."

I'm ... speechless.

"I hate Mom right now," Brian says.

"A couple at church ... ?" I prod.

"She *talked* to them!" he says, shaking his head in disbelief. "She talked to them about my baby!" He squeezes both hands into fists and shakes them. "If she ever, *ever* utters so much as a word about my baby to another living *soul*, I swear to god, I'll ... "

"It's okay, Bri," I say, rubbing his back.

"She will *never* see my baby," he mutters, his green eyes

glistening in the afternoon sun. "Olivia and I will leave town. We'll … "

"You're talking crazy, Brian. Mom … I know she's majorly annoying, but she isn't evil. I think she's just trying to sort all of this out."

"She's finished sorting," he snaps. "Got everything squared away, just like she was chairman of a bake sale. The last step was to break the news to Livy and me. Just one last little detail to take care of. Just a little blip on her radar before we returned to business as usual."

The waves are lapping farther from our feet, the tide sucking them away.

"I think she was just trying to make sure you know you have options," I say. "If adoption was the option you wanted to take, I guess she thought she was making things easier on you, coming up with a plan so you wouldn't have to … "

"To *what*?" he challenges, tossing a bitter glance at me. "To have to think too hard about which stranger to hand my kid off to? Does anybody in this family know me at all?"

I shake my head slowly. "This *is* a lot to take in."

"Yeah, well, get over it."

I flinch. He notices, then leans closer, his eyes locking with mine.

"Sorry," he says softly. "I know I've been snapping a lot lately." He picks up a sand dollar and fingers it gingerly. "It *is* a lot to take in. I know that. I hate that I laid all this on you guys, doing things bass-ackwards. It killed me to tell Mom; I knew it would break her heart. But then, when I told her...she was great, you know? I mean, she wasn't jumping for joy or anything, but she was staying calm, staying positive, saying it would all work out...I didn't know she was just biding time while she hatched her goddamn plot."

I nod. "Mom is a world-class plot hatcher," I muse, and when Brian laughs in spite of himself, I laugh with him.

"Remember when she tried to force me into piano lessons by telling me we were going to Mrs. Autry's house because she had a piano to sell?" I say. "Then, once we were there, if I wouldn't mind sitting down at the piano and trying it out? Then, next thing I know, Mrs. Autry is whipping out a book of scales."

Brian sputters with laughter. "She got me on the yearbook staff by telling me the advisor had cancer and needed my help," he says, his eyes twinkling.

"She *did* have cancer," I say. "That little mole on her upper lip? Basal cell."

We laugh some more.

"I hear it can be very debilitating," I continue earnestly. "When she had it removed, she had to wear a teeny little bandage for, like, two whole days."

Brian chortles. "Thank god I was there to help her through it. The club section might have pushed her over the edge if I hadn't been there to sort out the members in alphabetical order."

I breathe in the sea air. I love laughing with Brian like this.

He glances at me from the corner of his eye. "Thanks

for being so great to Olivia the past couple of days," he says. "It totally makes up for the crap you rained down on her for the last year."

I jab him playfully with my elbow.

"The way you guys hung out together today?" he says. "That was primo."

My gaze drifts down the beach. "Is she okay?" I ask.

Brian follows my gaze. "I better go catch up with her," he says. "Ya mind?"

"Nope," I say. "Hey, if she sees Church Lady chasing her with a net, tell her to run like hell."

Brian gives me a thumbs-up and starts trotting down the beach. My gaze follows his path for a couple of seconds, then I stare into the ocean, wiggling my toes in my damp tennis shoes.

God, Mom ... what were you thinking?

Then again, *of course* she was thinking about adoption. I was too! I mean, I hadn't exactly assembled the Potluck Supper Committee to set things in motion, but I sure wasn't ready to wrap my head around Brian being a father.

Until now.

Suddenly, his being a father seems like the most natural thing in the world. Of *course* he's going to raise his child. Of *course* he and Liv are going to be a family. If I ever had any doubt about that—or the slightest bit of doubt that he could pull it off—the last fifteen minutes wiped those thoughts entirely off the map.

I'm so proud of my brother. And, hey... I'm gonna be an aunt!

I squeeze my knees against my chest, a silly grin on my face, as I sense somebody on the beach inching closer to me. I ignore it at first—lots of people are milling around, after all—but, yes, somebody is definitely coming closer.

I shield my eyes with my hand, then look up. I squint to get a better look.

Oh.

"Hey, stranger."

seventeen

Scott kicks some sand idly with his bare foot. "You're not even gonna say hi?"

I shrug, still staring at the ocean. "Hi."

He sits next to me, letting his knee fall against mine.

"Not very friendly today," he says with a fake pout.

"Haven't seen a friend in a while."

"Ouch!" Even from my peripheral vision, I see him give an exaggerated wince. "I wanna be your friend."

Okay, the fake pouting is getting, like, nauseating.

The breeze blows a lock of hair onto my face. "I'd really like some privacy, if you don't mind . . ."

He leans closer and pulls the lock of hair away. "Don't be pissed," he coos into my ear. "*Pleeeeeeze?*"

I jerk my head away. "I don't even know you. Privacy, please?"

"You're pissed because I didn't talk to you the other

day," he says in a singsong voice, then fingers the same lock of hair he just pulled from my face.

I roll my eyes.

"I don't blame you," he says, still cooing, still fingering my hair. "I was just kinda caught off guard. I mean, I was in the middle of a game, and I couldn't exactly let on to my bros that this goddess on the beach has turned me into a puddle of sap."

He kisses my cheek before I can move away. "That's what you've turned me into, Forrest. A puddle of sap. I guess that's kinda fitting, huh? Forrest? Trees? Sap?"

I hold up my palm as a stop sign. "Do you *mind*?"

"Then, the rest of the week, my aunt had me painting her bathroom." He dangles a paint-flecked hand in front of my face. "See? Taupe, I think she calls it. Looks beige to me. Apparently there are, like, sixty-seven words for beige. Anyhow, she's making me put four coats of paint on her friggin' bathroom walls, and all I can think is, *Wonder what Forrest-like-the-trees is doing. Wonder if she's as drop-dead gorgeous today as she was before. Wonder if that walk on the beach made her stomach do somersaults like it did mine. Wonder if she'll bite my head off if I stop by and say hello.*"

I laugh a little in spite of myself, but I'm still staring straight ahead.

"A smile!" Scott nudges closer. I can feel his breath on my cheek. "Hot damn. I actually see a smile." He tugs lightly at my T-shirt. "Why ya wearin' shorts on the beach? And tennis shoes ... really wet ones ..."

I lift my chin. "I wear what I want."

"So how is it," he says, his voice husky, "that even wearing shorts and soggy tennis shoes, you're, like, a million times hotter than every other girl on the beach?"

For the first time since he's plopped down beside me, I turn to face him. "Do girls actually fall for these lines?"

He shrugs. "I don't care about any girls except one. I was kinda hoping *that* girl would fall for 'em ... fall for 'em like *timmmm-brrrrr.*"

As he says the word, his finger twirls slowly toward my chest, poking me in the heart on the last syllable.

"Fall for me, Forrest," he says softly, then leans in to kiss me.

My mind is swirling. I am *so* not falling for this. This guy is *so* not my type. I am *way* too mature for this...

Except that I'm kissing him back. As he presses his moist, salty lips against mine, I'm tilting my chin higher, nudging my face closer, tasting his tongue, panting lightly through my nose, resisting the urge to moan...

Who knew a first kiss could feel this natural?

Our faces move in a synchronized little dance, tilting right, left, right ... I'm barely even aware that he's shifting positions, putting his body on top of mine, holding my shoulders firmly but gently as he lowers my back against the sand, pressing his bare chest against my T-shirt...

My hands linger around his neck for a few moments, then slide downward and follow the curves of his biceps. His hands are pinned underneath me, but his torso pushes closer.

It's the sound of a couple of kids chortling that makes my eyelids flutter open. The kids are standing a few feet away, pointing and snickering. They're both boys, maybe twelve or thirteen. Our eyes meet, and I instinctively push Scott away.

"Noooooo . . ." he beseeches.

But I push harder, our tangled limbs beginning to disassemble. I point to the boys, who blush and skitter away.

"We need more privacy," Scott murmurs.

I push myself up on my elbows, then wipe sand from my arms.

"My aunt's going out to dinner in a while," Scott tells me, his eyes thick-lidded and his voice throaty. "I'll tell her I need to stay behind to finish painting the bathroom. We'll have the place to ourselves . . . at least for a couple of hours."

Um . . . um . . .

"I don't think so," I say, rising to my feet, my toes wriggling in my squishy shoes.

"Aw, c'mon . . ."

I wipe more sand off my body. "My family's going through some . . . stuff," I say. "Not tonight."

"But soon?" he prods, studying my face for an answer.

I just stand there. I don't know what to say.

Scott lowers his chin and looks up at me shyly. Then he winks, his deep-set eyes twinkly beneath a mop of sandy-blond hair.

"Yeah," he says. "Soon."

"Is it true?"

Dad looks up from his baseball game.

"Is it true that Mom is auditioning her church friends to adopt the baby?"

"*Forrest!*" Mom snaps, walking into the family room from the kitchen, a cheese grater in her hand.

"You had a family lined up for Brian's baby? The only thing left to do was break the news to him and Liv? Is it even *possible* to be that controlling?"

Dad lowers the volume on the game and pats the sofa for me to sit down, but I don't move.

I stare Mom down, expecting her to erupt in defiance. But instead, she stuns me by dissolving into tears.

Whoa. Mom *never* cries.

Dad walks over and hugs her loosely. "Can we dial it down?" he asks me.

"Sure," I say, planting my hands on my hips. "Once you guys stop blindsiding me with a secret du jour, I'll stop reacting with 'What the hell.'"

But my petulance is half-hearted. I hate seeing Mom cry. (Have I ever actually *seen* Mom cry before?)

Dad nudges her toward the couch, and they both sit down. I sigh, then plop in the easy chair next to them. "How could you have imagined Brian would ever be willing to give up a baby for adoption?" I ask Mom.

Her hand fumbles by her mouth.

Dad squeezes Mom closer. "Your mother was just trying to help ... to come up with some ideas, some options ... "

"Did Brian and Olivia ask for options?" I challenge.

"What do they know?" Mom asks through tears, her defiance roaring back. "They're eighteen! They can't know what it means to become parents!"

"No one can know until they do it," Dad says, trying to sound conciliatory but inciting Mom even more.

"We don't need platitudes, Michael! We need answers! We need a plan, a plan that will be in *everyone's* best interests, including *my grandchild's!*"

She crumbles into a fresh set of tears.

"But it's not your decision to make," I say quietly.

"Oh, thanks for the memo," Mom says, surprising me again. Sarcasm is rarely in her repertoire.

"But you had some *couple* lined up," I say, pitching forward.

"Oh, of course I didn't," Mom says dismissively, wiping her eyes. "It's common knowledge that this lovely couple in church can't have children and wants to adopt. I was just making mental notes. It's not like I was hustling them to an attorney's office in the dead of night."

I almost laugh in spite of myself. "Well, Brian is major-league pissed," I say instead.

"Oh, Forrest, you're just *full* of breaking news today," Mom says. Sarcasm again? I'm seeing whole new dimensions of my mother.

"Brian will be fine," Dad assures us. "Our conversation was just a little more . . . indelicate than we would've liked."

"I was plenty delicate," Mom says, narrowing her eyes

at him. "But what do *I* know? You two are obviously the experts on how to handle a family crisis."

"Just for future reference," I suggest, "let's file this away as Exhibit A of how *not* to do it." Dad chuckles, and a room full of tension suddenly seems to dissipate. Even Mom relaxes, leaning into his shoulder.

"You know, at work I get accolades all the time for my skills in crisis management," Mom says, and Dad and I exchange glances.

"Leave this one off your résumé, honey," he says, and we sputter with laughter. She picks up a throw pillow and bonks him over the head.

"Laugh all you want," she says, but her voice is light. "The cold hard fact is that we're *still* facing a world of problems. If you think Brian and Olivia are equipped at this point in their lives to go prancing merrily into some happily-ever-after future, then ... "

"I'll babysit!" I say, raising my hand.

Mom rolls her eyes. "God help us all."

———

"I met a guy on the beach."

Shelley gasps on the other end of the phone, and I cringe. Did I really just say that? What am I, twelve?

"Tell, tell!" she trills, and I stretch my legs out from the cedar chair on the deck, crossing them at the ankles.

"He's totally super cute," I say in a Valley Girl impersonation, and Shelley squeals.

"Who are you and what have you done with my best friend?" she asks.

"It's nothing," I say. "We just ran into each other a couple of times on the beach, and earlier today, we . . . "

"Eloped?" Shelley ventures.

"Yes, Shelley," I deadpan. "We're happily married now."

"What's his name?" she prods.

"Scott," I answer, a goofy smile spreading across my face.

"Scottie the Hottie! What does he look like?"

"Blond hair, green eyes, bulging biceps . . . "

She gasps. "I didn't know what you were gonna say was bulging."

I giggle. "He wanted me to hang out at his aunt's house tonight while she was at a restaurant. We would've had the place all to ourselves."

Pause.

"Okay, that's not a great idea," Shelley says, suddenly wary.

I narrow my eyes. "What? He just wanted to hang out."

"Take it slow, Forrest," she says. "He may have had something other than popcorn in mind."

I tsk. "We just met. God. What do you take me for?"

"A girl with a tragic dearth of experience in this area," Shelley says slowly.

"And you're worldly all of a sudden?"

"Worldlier than *you*, if you think that all the average guy wants to do is snuggle on the couch. Is that a word? 'Worldlier'?"

I'm feeling a little cornered all of a sudden. It was a big enough risk mentioning Scott in the first place without Shelley turning all schoolmarm on me.

"Invite him to have dinner with your family," she says.

"And then maybe Dad can take us to a matinee?"

"I'm serious, Forrest. Freaky things can happen on the beach."

"Oh, for crying out loud, I'm not twelve years old! Why did I even *tell* you this?"

"Because you like him," Shelley answers evenly. "You've hardly ever liked a guy enough to mention him to me, so if you're mentioning him, it's a big deal. And since you blew off Dating 101 while normal people were flirting with guys with braces at middle school dances, well ... you've skipped a few steps and you need to take it slow. That's all I'm saying."

I exhale through puffed-up cheeks. I shouldn't have called. It was stupid to mention Scott (it was one friggin' kiss, for crying out loud!) and I certainly can't tell Shelley what's going on with Brian, as much as I'm dying to, and since when did Shelley turn preachy? I really need to wrap this up.

"I better get going," I tell her.

"Hey, is it true that Olivia is bulimic?"

I roll my eyes. "Gotta go. I promised Dad a game of Scrabble."

"Now *that's* more your speed," she says, and though I know she's being silly, the remark still stings.

I'll choose my speed from now on, thank you very much.

eighteen

"Ya okay?"

This is the first chance I've had to talk to Olivia alone since our shopping trip.

"Yeah," she says from her bottom bunk. "I think Brian overreacted."

"Right," I say, staring at ceiling from my bed. "What's the big deal about promising your baby to some nice couple from church?"

She giggles. "That's what I mean. She never even *talked* to the couple from church. Brian didn't exactly get the facts straight."

I give a low whistle. "Mom's gonna love you," I say.

Pause.

"Not that it didn't hurt," Olivia concedes. "The fact that your mom thinks we would even *consider* giving our baby up for adoption ... yeah, that hurt. But she's had a lot to adjust to in the past few weeks."

"Whatever. People get pregnant every day, you know. It's not like she's dealing with an alien invasion. She's so naive. Mom has been way too sheltered all her life."

Crickets are chirping outside our bedroom.

"Your mom's a lot tougher than you think she is," Olivia says.

I pause, then ask, "What do you mean?"

"Nothing," she says quickly. "I'm just ... getting the impression that your mom is a lot stronger than she seems."

I knit my fingers together. "Today when I overheard Mom and Dad fighting ... "

"Yeah?"

"Mom was telling Dad he didn't get a vote about the baby."

Silence.

"What do you think she meant by that?" I ask.

More silence.

"And Dad said he didn't appreciate being treated like an outsider," I continue, not sure myself why I can't quite shake these words from my head. "An outsider."

Olivia says nothing.

"You know something I don't," I say, and even as I utter the words, I feel a strange sense of clarity. I'm just not sure what I'm clear about.

"What do you know?" I ask her, leaning up on an elbow.

"Nothing," Olivia murmurs unconvincingly.

I inch myself to a sitting position. "You do. You know something I don't." Our ceiling fan oscillates lazily overhead. "What do you know?"

When Olivia doesn't reply, I lean over my bunk and face her in the moonlight. "If you knew something, would you tell me?"

She swallows and averts her eyes. "Of course," she finally says, then locks eyes with me again. "I'm the BFF who took you bikini shopping, remember? Hey, you've *got* to wear that pink bikini tomorrow. It's supposed to be sunny all day."

I gaze at her for a moment, then plop back onto my bed. "I saw him today."

Olivia's mattress squeaks as she shifts in her bed. "The guy you took the walk with a few nights ago?"

"Yeah..." I finger a lock of hair. "We kinda...made out on the beach. Just for a couple of minutes."

God. I *am* twelve.

"Is it the first time you've kissed a guy?" Olivia asks.

"Of course not," I say, stunning myself by lying so effortlessly.

Olivia stands up and faces me. "I thought you said he blew you off when he was with his friends."

I nod quickly. "I know it was totally jerky, but he *did* kinda explain it. He said he was..."

"I don't care what he said," Olivia says disdainfully. "That's not okay, Forrest."

I shake my head. "No, really, it was just...it was just a misunderstanding. Then he spent the rest of the week painting his aunt's bathroom—he's staying at her beach house this summer—and ..."

"And you were making out?" Olivia prods.

"Just kissing."

"How old is he?" Olivia persists.

I'm embarrassed that I don't know, so here comes lie number two: "Seventeen."

Olivia runs a hand through her hair. "He sounds like a player, Forrest."

"He's actually very sweet," I say with an edge in my voice.

"No," Olivia says. "New guy. Tomorrow we find you a new guy."

I sit up abruptly, my legs dangling over the bed. "You sound like Shelley," I say. "What is it with you two? You find it totally inconceivable that a cute guy could be interested in me?"

Olivia's eyes widen. "No. *No!* I'm the one who told you how cute you are, how guys are always talking about how beautiful you are—"

"But not beautiful enough for any of them to ask me out," I say.

Olivia studies my eyes. "Did this guy ask you out?"

"Uh, *duh*," I say indignantly. "He asked me over to his aunt's house."

She nods, processing the information. "Like, for dinner with them?"

I huff. "Yeah. Something like that."

"*Something* like that?"

"God!" I punch my pillow. "Do I need a permission slip to have a conversation with a guy?"

"You didn't say anything about a conversation."

"Right," I snap. "He just walked up to me and started kissing me. And I'm such a pathetic sap that I was just like, 'Oooohh, sure, I'm a total loser who'll take whatever crumbs you toss my way.' Is that what you think of me?"

"I'm just trying to watch out for you . . . "

"Well, who asked you?"

She purses her lips and stares at the ground. "No one."

I take a deep breath. "I didn't mean to snap. Thanks for your concern. Really. But none of this is a big deal. He's a guy, that's all. I just wish people would give me a little more credit . . . or would think I'm entitled to a little attention." I swallow hard.

"That's not what I meant," Olivia whispers.

I nod. "Yeah. I know. Maybe we should just get some sleep."

But she lingers in her spot, still looking at me.

"We both need a good night's sleep," I say.

She pauses a moment more, then says, "Okay."

I turn to my side and stare at the wall. Maybe I *will* wear that pink bikini tomorrow.

———

I come home from school, walk into the den, let my backpack fall from my shoulders, and settle into the recliner as I turn on the TV. Then I grab my chemistry book and reach to the right to turn on the lamp so I can begin my homework.

Only the lamp's not there. That's weird. The lamp has been to the right of the recliner my whole life.

I glance around the room anxiously. Hey! I've suddenly noticed that lots of things are out of place. The coffee table is pushed up against a wall, and—what the hell—the couch is turned backward, away from the TV. Is this some kind of a joke?

Then Mom, Dad, and Brian walk into the room and settle onto the backward couch. Dad starts a crossword puzzle, and Mom and Brian are whispering to each other. I try to catch their eyes, but none of them notice me. Or maybe they do notice me and just won't acknowledge me.

"What's going on?" I practically shout.

Mom shushes me.

"Tell me!" I demand. "Everything is out of place! What's going on?"

"Nothing is 'going on,'" Mom says prissily.

"But the couch! It's turned backward! You're facing the wall! Why would you turn the couch backward?"

Mom, Dad, and Brian exchanges glances.

"What is going on?" I repeat frantically.

"Everything is fine," Dad says.

"No, it's not! Everything is weird!"

Then my dream gets even weirder: Scott walks in. At first, I'm excited; my heart actually skips a beat. But then I'm thinking, "You don't fit here; you don't fit."

But then, nothing fits anymore... right?

Scott walks over and squeezes into the chair beside me. Okay, this is a little too close for comfort; he's taking up so much room that I'm sinking into the chair cushion. I keep slipping farther and farther. I want to tell him "Hey, I'm disappearing into the chair," but I don't want to seem uncool, and everybody's acting like I'm the crazy one, and hey, maybe I am, so I keep my mouth shut as the cushion swallows me inch by inch until I'm suddenly gasping for air. Too late to speak up now.

nineteen

I pull my hair into a ponytail and lower my sunglasses.

It's noon. I've been on the beach all morning, and no Scott sightings. I think briefly about my dream the night before but literally shake it from my thoughts. It was just a stupid dream. So weird that Scott was in it...

Anyhow, it's not like I've been lying around all morning on the beach waiting for him. In fact, I've been in the middle of a good book, and I was relieved nobody bothered me while I finished it.

But I'm finished now.

Brian and Olivia are snoozing in the beach chairs next to mine, their fingers loosely interlocked. I put my book on my chair and head toward the surf.

It's so ridiculous that my heart is pounding. All I'm doing is taking a walk on the beach!

"Just taking a walk on the beach," I actually say to myself

out loud. No pep talks necessary, no explanations or justifications, no need for analysis... just taking a walk on the beach.

I kick beads of water as a wave skitters under my feet, then head east. I tug at my bikini bottom, force myself to stop *(this is how it's supposed to fit, moron)*, and swing my arms as I step into a loping stride. Swimmers and surfers thrash around in the ocean while kids dig in the sand and old people walk hand in hand.

I envy the old people, their flabby arms and doughy, dimpled thighs notwithstanding. *Their* hearts aren't pounding out of their chests. *Their* eyes aren't darting around wondering who may be looking at them and what those people may be thinking. They're simply ambling down the beach, enjoying the sea breeze, smiling at toddlers, pointing occasionally at sights of interest. Sometimes they're talking to each other, often not. If they have something to say, they say it, but silence is just fine too. Their relationships are as comfortable as a tattered terrycloth bathrobe. You like their floral one-pieces or the black socks their husbands wear with tennis shoes? Great. You don't? They couldn't care less.

This is Mom and Dad twenty years from now. Actually, it's Mom and Dad *today*, just without the dimpled thighs or black socks. That'll come; Mom's already complaining about wrinkles, and Dad's paunch gets a little paunchier each summer. They've long since settled into the rhythms of old-couple nonchalance. They've never struck me as deliriously in love, but they're as reliable and predictable as the tides. It's hard to imagine Brian and Olivia in these roles, but if they stand the test of time, they'll be the frumpy couple walking down the beach a few decades from now. Is that possible for them? Even though I've given Olivia short shrift the past few years (and the sudden realization that I may have inherited some of my mother's bitchiness is nothing short of mortifying), it's still hard to imagine her settling into long-term coupling, considering her background.

Dad said not to judge people by their parents, but how can Olivia commit to a long-term relationship when she's never seen one up close? Her dad seems pleasant enough, and kudos to him for sticking around when her mom bailed, but what happens if you don't have a built-in playbook when you get married? Being solid is probably the most natural thing in the world to Mom and Dad; both sets of my grandparents have been married for, like, eons. I know Olivia's heart is in the right place and her intentions are good, but does her relationship with Brian really stand a chance long term?

I really hope so. Now that we've ruled out handing their baby over to the lead alto and her earnest tenor husband in the church choir, I'm starting to feel what it will mean to have a baby in the family, to be an aunt, to watch Brian be a father. I want a perfect life for this baby. I want a niece I can spoil relentlessly, one I can teach to own the world and to never, ever feel excruciatingly self-conscious walking down the beach in her new pink bikini wondering if some guy she barely knows will notice, and...

And there he is. Just a few yards ahead of me, Scott is

playing Frisbee with his friends, just like he was a few days earlier. Oh god oh god oh god...

Don't mess this up, I tell myself, my heart pounding like a jackhammer. *Play it cool. No windmill arms or lame shout-outs. Play it cool.*

So I do. I just keep walking, grateful my sunglasses are obscuring my eyes. I swing my arms and tilt my chin skyward, just a girl minding her own business, walking on the beach, enjoying a sunny afternoon...

I don't slow my pace an iota as I walk past them. Still moving forward, still looking straight ahead, still just chillin'...

"Forrest!"

But I keep walking, acting like I didn't hear Scott calling my name.

"Forrest!" he repeats, louder this time.

I've passed him now, so I stop in my tracks, glance backward, adjust my sunglasses, toss him the subtlest of smiles, then flash him a peace sign. And keep walking.

"Hey!"

But I'm still walking.

"Wait up!"

I slow my pace and glance behind me, trying to look mildly annoyed. Scott is trotting up to me, his friends resuming their Frisbee game without him.

"That bikini is smokin' hot," he says, touching my forearm as he catches up with me.

"Thanks," I say coolly, still looking straight ahead. "Go finish your game."

Instead, he swoops closer and kisses my neck. "Frisbee seems awfully boring all of a sudden," he says.

I giggle. "I mean it. Go play. I just wanted some exercise."

He leans in to kiss me again on the neck, even though I haven't slowed my stride. "I can think of some other ways to get some exercise."

I giggle again. This is how guys talk, right? Granted, I can't imagine Dad or Brian talking this way, but who knows what kind of lines they used on girls back in the day. I mean, relationships have to start *somehow*, don't they? They don't just wash up on the beach fully formed.

Scott takes my hand and firmly pulls it toward him, forcing me to stop.

"Hey…" I whine playfully.

"Here's the thing," he says, pulling me close and staring in my eyes. "If you don't kiss me right now, I'm gonna be so bummed that I'll hurl myself into the ocean, and my foot is still bleeding from where I cut it on a seashell earlier today, so I'll probably be shark bait, and I'll—"

Then I kiss him. Just like that. It feels like the most effortless thing I've ever done. I kiss him, and he kisses me back, and my hands link around his neck, and he pushes closer, and we do that little face dance thing again—tilting left and right—and soon, he's pressing me so close that I can barely breathe.

"I… gotta go," I whisper when we finally pull our lips apart, our noses still nuzzling.

"Go where?"

I shrug. "I told you. I'm exercising."

"Baby, you're already a ten. Bodies don't get any hotter than yours."

I wrinkle my nose. "We can't stand here smooching all day."

"Oh, I definitely beg to differ." He leans in and kisses me again.

The waves lap at our feet. My hips sway. I love pink bikinis.

"Maybe you're right," Scott says after pulling away. "We can't stand here all day." He tosses his head toward the beach houses behind us. "Wanna come check out my aunt's house?" He raises a single eyebrow mischievously. "The guest bathroom is freshly painted."

Um...um...

"I dunno," I say coyly.

"Sure you do."

Okay, that's not a good idea. Take it slow, Forrest.

He sounds like a player, Forrest. New guy. Tomorrow we find you a new guy.

Okay, Shelley and Liv, you can get out of my head now. Four's a crowd.

"C'mon..." Scott is cooing, pulling me farther up the beach.

"Um...I've got a better idea."

"Yeah?"

"My house. Come to my house for dinner tonight. You can meet my family."

Scott's face is inscrutable.

"*Come*," I prod. "I want you to meet my brother. You two have a lot in common."

Okay, that sounds stupid, considering that the sum total I know about Scott is that he likes Frisbee and can paint a bathroom. But still...

"Dinner..." he says, rubbing the back of his neck.

"My mom is highly annoying, but she's an awesome cook."

He squints into the sun. "What time?"

"Seven. My house is the one with the—"

"You think I don't know which house is yours?" he says, grinning.

I lean closer and give him a peck on the cheek. "Seven at my house. Now, lemme finish my walk, for crying out loud."

He squeezes my hands, then trots back toward his friends.

My heart feels like it's about to leap from my throat onto the beach.

Seven at my house. That has the most incredible ring to it.

twenty

"I told you: it's just a friend."

"Well, what's your friend's name?" Mom asks, her hands on her hips.

Damn. Did I really think this through, pulling Nosy Nora into my romance?

"Scott," I say, then feel my heart sink as Mom's eyes widen dramatically.

"A boy."

"Mom, please don't make this a bigger deal than it is," I plead. "He's just a nice guy I invited over for dinner."

Mom reaches into a plastic bag to continue putting her groceries away. "Of course," she says, pulling out a can of diced tomatoes. "Your friends are always welcome."

"What are you cooking?" I ask anxiously.

"I was planning on meat loaf..."

"Mom, *please* not meat loaf."

Mom sets the jar of tomatoes on the kitchen counter. "What did you have in mind?"

I shrug. "Do you know how to make lobster?"

"Lobster?"

"Or shrimp, then. Maybe shrimp pasta?"

Mom's eyebrows crinkle. "I'd have to head right back out to the store..."

I sigh with relief. "Perfect. Thank you, Mom. Need some help putting the groceries away?"

"Well, considering that I'm headed right back out..."

"Leave it to me."

Mom studies me for a second, then picks up her purse.

"Pasta and a salad... is that all right?" she asks.

"Perfect."

I impulsively kiss her on the cheek, and she heads back out the door.

I walk through the family room to the deck, where Dad is reading a book.

"Imbroglio," he says, not looking up as I join him.

"Like, a big mash-up of confusion," I say.

"You must have been studying a dictionary. Webster precedes lots of definitions with the word 'like.'"

I wink and sit beside him. "You're just mad you can never trip me up. I have, like, the gigantic-est vocabulary ever."

Dad sets his book aside and stretches his legs out. "Things settling down with Mom and Brian?" he asks.

"Brian says she'll never lay eyes on his baby, but other than that..."

"So they've basically patched things up."

"I dunno … it's quite the imbroglio," I say, messing with Dad by pronouncing the *G*. I tap a finger against my thigh for a couple of moments, then add, "Oh, by the way, a friend is coming over for dinner tonight."

Dad raises an eyebrow. "A friend."

"Yeah. No biggie."

"A friend from home?"

I sigh, exasperated. "No, Dad. Just a friend. Like I said, no big deal."

"Well, does the friend have a name? Or should I just say, 'Hi, Friend'?"

"Scott. His name is Scott."

Dad takes that in, then nods slowly, staring at the beach.

"A new friend?" he finally asks.

"Just a friend, Dad. Can we not make this a big deal?"

"Like, an imbroglio?" he says, messing back by pronouncing the *G*.

"Funny."

"So," Dad says, practically doing backflips to try to sound casual, "this Scott is a nice guy?"

I huff. "Why is so inconceivable to everybody that a guy might be interested in me?" Uh-oh. I'm trying to keep things casual, and here I go casting myself as a needy loser.

"I just asked if he's nice," Dad says, holding up his hands in self-defense. "And by the way, nothing seems less inconceivable to me than a guy thinking you're the most spectacular girl on earth."

Oh god.

"You know," Dad continues, still staring at the ocean, "I hardly dated at all before I met your mom."

I wish I could shift the conversation back to vocabulary words, but I guess it's too late for that now.

"Yeah?" I say, feigning indifference.

"Yeah. I was always really shy around girls. Plus, I think it's well established what an outstanding student I was, and, you know, *that* takes lots of time."

I snicker. "So you were shy around women, but Mom, of all people, was the one you finally felt comfortable enough with to ask out?"

"Oh, no," he responds. "Nothing about your mom made me comfortable. She scared the bejeesus out of me. So pretty and confident..."

"So why her?" I ask.

He shrugs. "My interest outweighed my fear. I'd had my eye on her a long time...kept trying to be at the right place at the right time, dropping all kinds of hints...but she wasn't interested in some guy loitering on the sidelines. I had to get in the game to stand a chance with her."

"So you finally asked her out?"

"Yeah. I finally asked her out."

"And you swept her off her feet?"

His eyes turn wistful. "Your mom's not a swept-off-her-feet kinda gal. But it was enough. Whatever I had to offer was enough."

I lean closer to him. "Dad, you're way more than enough."

His expression lightens. "Tell her that for me, will you? And while you're at it, mention I'm really hungry for meatloaf."

I grimace. "Sorry. I kinda ruined that for you. Is shrimp pasta okay instead?"

He pouts. "The girls always get their way around here."

I stand up and tap his knee before walking back inside. "Yeah, and don't you forget it."

———

"A guest for dinner, huh?"

I swat Brian with the kitchen towel. "This is why I don't date."

"Looks like you're dating now," Brian says in a sing-song voice.

Olivia walks into the kitchen. "Who's dating?"

"Forrest has a 'friend' coming over for dinner," Brian answers, with elaborate air quotes around "friend."

Olivia sucks in a breath. "The guy from the beach?" she asks me.

I roll my eyes. "A friend is coming over for dinner. That's it. Don't you think I have my hands plenty full keeping Mom in line? Just be cool, okay, guys? Please? For me?"

"When did you invite him?" Olivia asks.

"I didn't *invite* him," I snap. "I just said, you know, like, 'Hey, we'll be eating dinner around seven if you wanna come.'"

"Now, granted, my vocab can't compete with yours, but I'm pretty sure that qualifies as an invitation," Brian says. "And you're sure he actually RSVP'd...?"

He's teasing, but my stomach is tied in too many knots to play along. Scott will be here in less than an hour. I've already helped Mom peel the shrimp, so now I have to go shower the fishy smell out of my pores and decide what to wear.

"What are you gonna wear?" Olivia says. I swear, it's like people are reading my thoughts these days.

"Just *whatever*," I say.

Brian snorts. "Like you haven't thought about it."

"Wanna borrow something of mine?" Olivia asks.

I squeeze my hands into fists. "You guys! Please just cool it, okay? I'm capable of having a friend over for dinner without a team of advisors." I glare at Brian. "Or smartasses."

"Well, if I *was* advising you," he says, "I'd definitely suggest showering. You smell like shrimp."

I stick out my tongue and leave the kitchen. Olivia follows me down the hall.

"Hey, Forrest?"

Oh please don't make me keep talking about this. I'll barf, I swear I will.

"Yeah?"

"I just... I'm glad he's coming to dinner. I know you like him, and that's great. I was just a little worried, based on... well, you know. But if he's coming to dinner and meeting your family, well, that's great."

I manage a tight smile. I know she means well, but geez,

I'm sick of being under a microscope. "Thanks. I'm gonna grab a quick shower."

"Right. And I meant what I said … about borrowing an outfit, if you want. I could help you pick one out … "

"I'm cool. Really. But thanks."

"Right."

Olivia smiles and heads back toward the kitchen.

Maybe the knot in my stomach will unravel by the time Scott gets here.

twenty-one

"What is an oligarchy?"

"What is an oligarchy?" the *Jeopardy!* contestant on TV says, and Dad smiles. He's always a step ahead of the *Jeopardy!* contestants.

His rat-a-tat answers are the only thing lifting the tension in the room as the moments tick away. At first, we all tried to act casual; seven o'clock came and went, but, whatever, lots of people show up late for a dinner date. Then, at ten after seven, it was like, no big deal, Scott will be here any minute. Then ten more minutes... then another ten... then *Jeopardy!* started, along with Mom's questions about whether my "friend" was sure which house was ours...

And maybe he's not. Scott *said* he knew where I lived, but I never gave him the address, and he doesn't have my phone number in case he needed to call, and...

And nothing. Every neighbor within a mile knows us, so

if he went to the wrong house, somebody would immediately point him in the right direction. He's had time to find me.

He just doesn't want to.

I guess he never had any intention of coming. But in that case, why not just say so?

I can't believe my stupidity. He blows me off once, then I give him a chance to do it again? A few kisses on the beach and I think we're some sort of couple? Never a single real date, yet I blithely assume he'd jump at the chance to spend an evening with my parents? I'm the loser of the universe.

The only thing worse than the pity I feel emanating from my family's pores is the fact that they're trying so hard not to show it. Just hanging out, watching *Jeopardy!*, ready to eat cold pasta whenever I give the word, but no rush, no biggie...

I'd go collapse on my bed if I could, but that would just add more layers of awkwardness, more hushed conversations about who should go check on me, more forced cheerfulness to make sure I'm clear that being stood up on my first real date is *no big deal*.

So all I can do is sit there and listen to Dad answer the *Jeopardy!* questions while stomachs grumble around me. Seriously, I'm no drama queen, but there is no form of death right now I wouldn't welcome. After all, I have to survive not only *this* excruciating moment, but every moment for the rest of my life hereafter with this searing humiliation looming sadistically in my memory bank. I'd throw confetti on the Grim Reaper if he walked in right now.

Bang! Bang! Bang!

We all exchange startled glances. It's weird that Scott is banging on our front door rather than merely ringing the doorbell, but omigod I am so relieved he's here that I could cry. *He's here! He came! I'm not the most pathetic person on the face of the earth!*

Bang! Bang! Bang!

Mom is heading for the door when it suddenly flings open.

"Where is she?!? Where is my daughter?!?"

We're all on our feet now, rushing toward the foyer. We're so ridiculously disoriented that the woman on the doorstep stops ranting long enough to absorb our stunned expressions.

But just for a moment. Now she's ranting again: "I want my daughter NOW!"

"Mom!" Olivia gasps, lunging to her side. "What are you *doing?*"

"I'm taking you home!"

The woman flings her arms around Olivia's neck, sobbing as their long blonde hair intertwines.

We stand there for a moment exchanging what-the-hell looks, then Dad prods mother and daughter inside and closes the door behind them.

"Why don't we all sit down ... " he says.

"I don't want to sit down!" Olivia's mother shrieks. "I'm taking my daughter home this instant!"

Olivia disentangles from her mother's embrace. "Mom, what are you doing?"

"I told you! I'm taking you home! We're not spending another minute around these maniacs trying to steal your baby!"

Brian's back stiffens. "What home are you talking about?" he asks her. "You've never made a home for Olivia in your life!"

"Don't even think about turning this around on me!" the woman shouts, shaking a finger at him. "You're probably in on your mother's plan: 'Find some couple at church to adopt the little bastard, Mom, but act like I don't have anything to do with it. Then maybe I can keep getting all the sex I want after this little inconvenience is taken care of.' Well, you're not getting off that easy, buddy! I'll make sure you fulfill your responsibility to your baby if it's the last thing I do!"

"Like you fulfilled yours?" Brian yells, his eyes bulging.

"Stop it, stop it!" Olivia cries. She gives Brian a pleading look. "I called her yesterday, right after you told me about the conversation with your parents, when I was still upset and didn't realize—"

"Didn't realize *what?*" Olivia's mother says. "That the only reason this woman invited you to her froufrou beach house was to steal your baby out from under you?"

Mom presses a hand against her cheek, her mouth agape.

"She was just trying to give us some options," Olivia says, tears streaming down her cheeks. "She wasn't trying to ram anything down our throats. I didn't understand. Like I said, I called you when I was still upset, and—"

"Well, I'm pretty damn upset right this minute!" her mother shoots back.

Dad holds a palm in the air. "Hold it! Everybody needs to calm down. Please!"

"What do *you* have to say about anything?" the mother says, sneering at Dad. "Speaking of which, I want genetic testing done on this baby. No telling what kind of medical history we'll be dealing with."

Stunned silence.

Olivia locks teary eyes with Brian and mouths, "*I'm sorry.*"

As my eyes dart from one face to the next, the realization shoots through my heart like a dagger: my imagination *hasn't* been running wild. My instincts *aren't* off base.

Everybody knows something I don't.

twenty-two

Nobody moves a muscle.

My mind is reeling, and everyone else seems like they've just been thwacked in the head with a two-by-four.

Genetic testing...

Medical history...

"Get. Out. Of. My. HOUSE!" Mom's roar thunders through the foyer like a tsunami. "OUT!"

"Honey..." Dad cajoles, but Mom waves him away like a gnat.

"You will not waltz in here and tear my family apart," Mom tells Olivia's mother. "*Get the hell out!*"

Every jaw drops. Mom is actually shaking. And cursing! This is surreal.

Olivia's mother is frozen in place.

"Out!" Mom shrieks, lunging toward her.

"Hold it!" Brian interjects, stepping between the two

mothers and making a time-out motion. He glances at Olivia. "Let's take your mom out and get some fresh air."

Olivia nods, her eyes petrified.

"Who are you to kick me out?" Olivia's mom sputters, indignant to be out-bullied.

"I will tear your hair out if you hurt my family," Mom responds, in the most chilling monotone I've ever heard.

"We're leaving, we're leaving," Brian says, taking Olivia and her mother by their arms. "We'll get some air, get a bite to eat, we'll calm down, then we'll..."

Then we'll what? Watch these two banshees claw each other's eyes out?

"Then we'll discuss this like adults," Brian finishes.

That's just what Brian suddenly seems like. An adult. I know he is one now, technically speaking, but up until this beach trip it's been hard to see him as anything other than the kid who played SpongeBob to my Sandy Cheeks in our backyard games as toddlers. Maybe that's why it's been so hard to picture him as a father. Suddenly, it's not hard at all. I swallow hard.

Brian leads Olivia and her mother outside, then closes the door behind him.

My parents and I stand there, the tension of the past few moments seeping out like steam from a teakettle.

twenty-three

"It's time."

Mom shakes her head, squeezing her eyes shut.

"Maureen: it's time."

Approximately three minutes have passed since I've exhaled. Looking from Mom's frantic face to Dad's expression of sad resignation has convinced me of one thing: my dread now firmly outweighs my curiosity. Whatever it's time for, I don't think I want to know.

Dad looks at me. "Let's sit down, honey."

But I don't move a muscle until he takes my arm and leads me toward the family room.

"Michael..." Mom protests weakly, but she follows us to the couch. Mom and I sit on it—collapse on it, really—and Dad sits across from me in the recliner, pitching forward and putting his hand on my knee.

"Honey..."

Mom moans, dropping her face into her palms.

"Honey, you know how much your mother and I love you and Brian ... " Dad continues, and a thousand Very Special Episodes of saccharine sitcoms fill my head.

"Nothing could ever change that," he adds, and I wonder if the nervous tension will make me burst into hysterical laughter. But I just keep sitting there, waiting for the shoe to drop.

"Honey, when your mother and I—"

"No!" Mom wails, her face still buried in her hands.

Dad pauses a moment, then continues: "When we—"

"NO!" Mom says again. "I mean it, Michael! I can't do this! We need time to ... "

"To *what*?" Dad challenges, kind but resolute.

"To do this right!"

Dad moves his hand from my knee to Mom's. "It's time," he whispers.

Mom jumps to her feet. "I can't! Do you understand that? I can't!"

She runs down the hall and slams her bedroom door behind her.

We hear her weeping, and Dad looks torn for a moment about whether to go to her. But his mind is made up. He's clearly decided there's no turning back now.

He clears his throat and seems to force himself to hold my gaze. "When your mother and I started dating," he says, absurdly trying to sound casual, "she was already pregnant."

I'm still staring at him as if he's just uttered something in a foreign language. "Pregnant."

He nods. "Right, sweetie. She was already pregnant."

"But ... how did you get her pregnant if you weren't dating yet?"

Okay, I'm fully aware of how stupid that sounds, and I don't recall actually forming the question in my brain, but somehow, those are the words that fall from my mouth.

Because that's the only explanation I can absorb: that Dad got Mom pregnant.

"Um ... " Dad says, looking around the room for a moment before homing in again on me. "I wasn't the one who got her pregnant."

Oh.

My eyebrows knit together, my mouth open as if awaiting a fresh jumble of stupid words to fall out. "What happened to the baby?"

Dad's eyes fall. "The baby is your brother."

Oh. I have a brother I didn't know about? Wait, no ...

"Brian," I say, surprising myself by sounding eerily matter-of-fact.

But that can't be, so I'm really eager for Dad to explain what's *really* going on and why there's no reason to believe my world has just been shattered and why this whole thing is a giant misunderstanding and ...

"Right," Dad says. "Brian."

He holds my hand between both of his. I pull it away.

"Brian's … not your son." My voice is so flat, I wonder if I said the words aloud or just thought them.

"Of *course* he's my son," Dad says, and I think, *Whew, my world is still on its axis after all! I've just misunderstood…*

But then I get it. Brian is Dad's son in a Very Special Episode kind of way. As in, not at all.

"You're not his dad."

I'm talking to myself now, just trying to take it all in.

Dad grabs my hands, holding them too tightly to let me pull them away. "I've loved your brother since the moment he was born … since *before* he was born. He's my son as surely as if—"

"She's such a hypocrite," I say to myself in barely a whisper, peering blankly into space. "Such a friggin' hypocrite…"

"*No.* Your mother is *not* a—"

"She was using you," I say in a monotone. "She's still using you."

"Forrest, you *know* your mother and I love each other very—"

"You said it yourself," I say, pulling my hands away and rising to my feet. "You said you tried forever to get her to go out with you, but she wasn't interested until…"

"That's *not* what I meant, Forrest."

But I'm already heading toward the back door.

"Forrest, wait!"

What a Very Special Episode thing to say.

"Wait!" Dad repeats as I fling the door open. He's caught up with me by the time I've reached the stairs of our deck.

"I need some time," I tell him, aiming for calm to increase the odds that he'll leave me alone.

"Honey, you don't understand ... "

"Please, Dad? Just a little time to myself?"

He stands there looking torn, then finally nods. "Please hurry back ... so we can all talk."

Yeah, that'll give me something to look forward to.

"You really haven't heard the ... "

But I'm already running down the steps, toward the beach, away from my dad.

He *is* my dad, right?

Who the hell knows? Suddenly, everything I've ever believed, everybody I've ever trusted ... it's all up for grabs, a giant crapshoot, just a big, heapin' helpin' of *shit*.

By the time my sneaker-clad feet hit the sand, I'm running, running somewhere, running toward the water, I guess, I dunno, I don't care, just running...

People are milling around me—dusk is just setting in and a peachy sunset is piercing through billowy clouds— but I'm oblivious, still just running, just pushing forward, wondering if I can outrun the sound in my head of my life splintering into a million pieces. I run until I hit the surf, then fall onto the wet sand, holding my head in my hands as the lazy, rippling waves of low tide nibble at my sneakers.

I'm vaguely aware of the outfit I'm wearing—the snug shorts, the B-52s T-shirt (campy, ironic, understated—like I've coolly thrown on the first thing I grabbed from the drawer)—and cringe as I remember I picked it out specifically for Scott.

Scott. That guy from a lifetime ago. The one from a parallel universe. The one who stood me up a mere hour ago. The one I gave a shit about before I realized I had *real* problems. The one who made sense in my world when my world wasn't full of deception. Thirty sunsets, my ass. Thirty zillion *lies*. And counting.

Fitting, no? Scott's done apparently nothing but lie the whole time I've known him, and my family has done nothing but lie the whole time I've known *them*, with me going about my business ludicrously believing what I was told, inexplicably trusting people, imperviously living my life as if I had a goddamn clue.

They've all been lying to me... even Brian.

Because Brian knows. *I'm sorry*, Olivia mouthed to him when her mom blathered about genetic testing. *I'm sorry I told my mom what everyone on earth besides your idiot sister has apparently known forever, that you're not who she thinks you are, that she's not who she thinks she is, and that, oh by the way, I'm your confidante now, not your what's-her-name sister. Half sister, that is.*

How could Brian know this without telling me? Haven't we always told each other everything? He's the only one I ever told about my weird OCD habit of alternating which side of my teeth I brush first—left to right in the morning, right to left at bedtime—one of a million ways I'm committed to an insane notion of symmetry. I'm the only one who ever heard

Brian's confession that it was him, not his friend Ty, who accidentally ripped the upholstery of a new chair the very day Mom bought it.

Sure, our relationship took a sharp turn south when Olivia came on the scene, but at least *that* was a betrayal that fell within the parameters of a world that made sense.

This ... *this* betrayal ... a betrayal that makes a mockery of every single moment of my childhood, my life up to this point, considering that it was all based on a lie—*this* defies the very laws of physics.

I feel my heart pounding through my B-52s T-shirt.

"Damn, where's my sunscreen?"

What?

I look up and see Scott.

Oh my god.

He pretends to wipe his brow. "All your hotness is giving me a sunburn." He ludicrously draws out of the *R*s on *burrrn*.

"Please go away."

Scott drops to one knee and peers into my eyes. "Slather some sunscreen on me, baby."

I gaze past him into the ocean. I don't even have the energy to tell him to go to hell.

"Whatcha pissed about?" he asks, then draws in a quick breath. "Hey, wait ... that dinner with your family ... that wasn't supposed to be *tonight*, was it?"

I'd give my right arm if I could summon a mythical sea creature to swallow this joker whole right about now.

He slaps the side of his head. "It *was* tonight! Why was

I thinking you said tomorrow? Damn! I've definitely been sniffing too much paint. Oh, baby, look, I'm so—"

"I really need my privacy right now. Please leave me alone."

"Oh, *please*, baby, you gotta give me another chance. Hey, I know how to make it up to you. *I'll* cook dinner for *you*..."

Damn.

I'm crying now.

I absolutely hate crying in front of this moron, making him think I care about some damn *dinner*, giving him the impression that he's so much as a blip on my radar screen. But there you have it. I'm sitting in the sand crying. I wipe my tears roughly with the heel of my hand.

"Oh, baby, don't cry."

I swear to god, if Scott calls me baby one more time, I will shove a jellyfish up his nose.

"It was an honest mistake, baby," he says, and honestly, where's a jellyfish when you need one?

I glance up at him. "This really isn't about you," I say. "I've got some family stuff going on right now. A little privacy? Please?"

"Are you *sure* you didn't say tomorrow? I could have *sworn* it was tomorrow that I was supposed to—"

"Scott." I look squarely in his eyes. "I really need to be alone right now." I stand up and start walking toward my house.

"Baby!" Scott beseeches. "It was an honest misunderstanding! Can't a guy make a single mistake? *Jesus.* What are *you*, Queen Perfect? Never made a single mistake yourself? Never got a date wrong? Must be nice to be so goddamn … "

My walk turns into a trot; I'm desperate to distance myself from the sound of his voice, the smugness on his stupid face.

"Yeah, run, Little Miss Perfect!" he shouts angrily. *He's* angry? God, this is rich.

"You *better* run!"

What the hell does that mean? Not that I care.

"You little bitch!"

Did he really just say that? I quicken my pace.

Then I hear the thud of bare feet running on the sand. And getting closer.

Oh god. He's running after me.

I'm more mad than scared. The *nerve* of this guy! Is he *serious*? Has a bigger jerk ever walked the face of the—

He grabs my arm from behind.

His eyes flash with anger as he jerks me toward him, but then he turns cajoling again. "Don't be mad. I'm still thinking about you in that pink bikini. You can't do that to a guy—look so smokin' hot and then cut him loose."

"Let me go."

His eyes flash with fury as his chin pitches forward.

"Scott, lemme—"

But his grip tightens.

"You're hurting me."

My eyes scan the beach. A few people are around, but none close enough to summon without making a scene.

And that would be ridiculous, right? To make a scene just because some jerk is...

I gulp as I realize he's pulling me toward a canopy-covered gazebo, one of those flimsy little structures moms prop on the beach to keep their babies in the shade. Flimsy, but private. Once the flap of the canopy is closed, no one can see inside. No one can...

Scott pulls me inside, closes the flap, presses his face against mine, and starts kissing me.

I push him away. "Let me *go*."

"C'mon, baby," he murmurs, "don't be mad. Let's make up."

I try to protest, but he's pressing his mouth tightly against mine, his tongue probing as I start to gag and push harder against his chest.

He's panting, his hands sliding down my waist, his fingers digging into my flesh, and I feel faint as I try but fail to gasp for oxygen.

Finally, I shove him with the palms of my hands as hard as I can. He stumbles, but his arms still have me in a vise grip.

A bulging vein in his neck throbs. His eyes look wild and enraged, yet cold and calculating. Like an animal's. He roughly pulls me closer and starts kissing me again.

I consider squealing as loud as I can with his face pressed against mine. But would anyone hear? And even if they did, would they realize I was in trouble, or just assume I was horsing around on the beach? Should I try to bite his lip? I'm not sure I can, and even if I could, would it just enrage him more?

Of course it would. If nothing else is clear to me right now, I have perfect clarity that Scott will accept nothing less than complete control.

He's trying to yank down my shorts, but he's struggling to hold me still at the same time. He eases off a bit, redistributing his weight.

"Please don't..."

His eyes narrow, staring at me.

"You're hurting me," I continue. "Please don't hurt me."

His eyes flash hesitation for a nanosecond, then go cold. "Just go with it," he demands.

"Not like this," I plead, desperate not to further incite him. If I can just keep him calm...just remind him that I'm a person, like his mother or sister...

"You're really hurting me," I tell him again, trying to make eye contact.

"Then hold still. I got no time for goddamn teases."

"Then let's do this right," I whisper in rapid-fire pants.

He studies me warily, then gives a creepy smile and starts to lower me to the ground.

"No!" I yelp, struggling to stay on my feet. "I don't mean now. Don't you want to make it special for me? I've never done this before. I don't want it like this, not in the sand. Besides, somebody might come back. I saw a mother and her kids just a minute ago, looking for shells. I think this is their—"

"Nobody's coming," he says contemptuously.

"No, really! I saw the mom and her kids here earlier today.

This is their gazebo; I'm sure of it. And they were just on the beach. I'm sure they'll be back any minute. I think they—"

"Shut *up*," he says, then shoves me hard onto the sand.

I try to lift myself up on my elbows, but he's already on top of me, pinning me to the ground.

"Scott," I mutter, pushing my face to the side. "I have a venereal disease."

He laughs coldly. "You just said you were a virgin."

"It's ... AIDS ... from a blood transfusion ... "

"Lying bitch," he says, then yanks my head back into position so he can kiss me. He's biting my lower lip, still digging his fingers into my flesh, making me gasp for air again ... oh god oh god oh god ... I shut my eyes tight and summon every ounce of energy I have, then ...

Oooooomph!

Scott's eyes widen, then squeeze shut as he moans in pain, gripping the testicles I've just crushed with my knee. I push him off of me, fling open the flap of the canopy, and run like hell.

twenty-four

Is Scott behind me?

I don't know; the only thing I'm conscious of is the sound of my own heaving breaths. I can't pause to look behind me. *Keep moving forward... keep moving forward...*

Should I be screaming? I don't know if I can; I don't think I have enough oxygen to do anything except keep running. My sneakers pound the sand—*slap, slap, slap, slap*—and my breaths course through me like hot lava. If people are around, I'm oblivious. *Just keep moving toward the house...*

I push past marram grass and feel insanely relieved when I reach the other side, as if a border of waist-high, wisp-thin grass is going to shield me from harm. But I'm still push-ing forward, running as fast as I can, pumping my forearms, inhaling oxygen in convulsive gulps. I reach the stairs of our deck and climb them two at a time. It's only when I reach the landing that I glance anxiously toward the beach.

No one is in sight. Scott hasn't followed me … unless he's lurking somewhere out of sight, ready to pounce when I least expect it. I have a sudden sick feeling that I'll never rest easy another moment of my life, forever vigilant against the possibility of being pounced on unexpectedly.

But I'm safe now, just a few steps away from my back door, a few steps away from Mom and Dad, a few steps away from shedding the most profound sense of aloneness I've ever felt. *Mom and Dad, mind if I hold your hands for the rest of my life?*

I practically collapse against the back door, then reach for the knob to open it.

Oh god … it's locked.

I glance anxiously toward the beach again as I start slapping the door furiously. It occurs to me that slapping the door this hard should hurt my hand, but nothing hurts—not my red palms, not my exhausted lungs, not my shaky thighs. My only focus is on getting inside.

I see Mom and Dad rushing toward the door through the windows, and I've never been so glad to see them in my life. What if they hadn't been home? What if I'd been stuck outside this locked door, knowing Scott could spring on me at any moment? I think my heart would have exploded with fear. Literally exploded. I believe that now—that a heart can explode with fear.

"Forrest, what in the world … ?" Mom is saying.

"Rape … rape … " I gasp. "He tried to rape me."

Dad holds my arms to steady me and looks deep into my eyes. "Who tried to rape you?"

"Scott... the guy who was supposed to... oh god, he tried to *rape* me..."

"What does he look like?" Dad asks me, his voice steady yet menacing.

I shake my head. "*Look* like? I don't know... he's... does it matter? I'm sure he's gone by now."

Dad looks at Mom. "I'm calling the police," he says.

"No!" I cry.

But Dad's already reaching for his cell phone.

"Dad! Nothing happened! I don't even know his last name..."

He's pressing numbers on his phone pad.

"Dad! Please!"

He pauses and looks at me. "He tried to rape you."

"Yes, but... I got away. Nothing happened. Please, Dad, nothing happened!"

He resumes pressing numbers. Oh god. Oh god oh god oh god...

"Forrest," Mom says, pulling my arm.

"No!" I shriek, but Mom won't let go. She's pulling me toward her, then pulling me down the hall to my bedroom. I'm too weak and disoriented to resist.

Once inside the bedroom, Mom lowers me to the bottom bunk. I sprawl on the mattress, spent and exhausted. Mom lies down behind me and wraps her arms around me. I should sob now... right?

Right. I should sob. I want to sob. My brain has hit the "sob" button of my limbic system, so why am I not sobbing? Nothing would feel better right now than to vomit out my emotions in a steady stream of wails.

But I'm not sobbing. I'm just lying there, clutching my mother's arms.

"What happened?" she asks softly.

"Nothing." My chest is still pounding, but my voice is flat, lifeless.

"You can tell me, Forrest."

"You wouldn't understand."

Mom pulls me gently up by my arms, then coaxes me onto my feet despite my wobbly legs. She stands in front of me, steadying my shoulders. "Tell me what happened."

Okay, *now* the sob sequence has been activated. I fall into her arms and weep on her shoulder, my body shaking against hers. I cry for a long time as Mom strokes my hair, murmuring into my ear that everything will be okay. Dad pokes his head in the door at some point, nods at Mom, then shuts the door behind him.

Mom lowers me to the bed again, sitting beside me as she squeezes my hand and peers into my eyes.

"What happened? The boy who was supposed to come to dinner tonight ... that's who it was?"

A fresh wave of tears rolls down my cheeks.

"He tried to rape me, Mom. He got me alone in this gazebo-type thing on the beach, and he wouldn't let me go."

I glance at her, expecting her to wince and look away, but she holds my gaze. "Did he hurt you?"

I shake my head, then hold it still, then nod. "He shoved me, he bit me..."

Yes. He hurt me.

"But... you got away?" Mom leans in closer, tightening her grip on my hand.

I nod, sniffling. "The knee... I used my knee."

"Good girl. I'm so proud of you. This won't go unanswered, Forrest."

"Mom, no," I moan. "I don't want to talk to anybody about it. I never want to see him again. I don't even know his last name... I don't know where he lives... oh god, it would be his word against mine... no!"

I start crying again, and Mom gathers me in her arms the way she gathers laundry, all bundled and compact, ready to be taken care of.

"I know you're upset," she says in an eerily calm voice, "but what he did is against the law. This is a criminal matter."

I squeeze more tears from my eyes and shake my head against her chest. "I'm so stupid. Stupid, stupid, stupid."

"You're not stupid," Mom says firmly. "I'm so sorry he hurt you."

"I'm sixteen," I say. "Most girls have had experience with guys by my age. And I don't even know a nice guy from a..."

"A rapist," Mom says.

I shake my head. "But there more to it than that. You don't understand, Mom. I... we kissed on the beach a couple of times, and as stupid as it sounds, that was cool with me. I *liked* him. And I guess he thought I was becoming, like, I dunno, his girlfriend or something..."

"You're entitled to kiss a guy without him forcing himself on you," Mom says. "He tried to rape you, Forrest. And that doesn't make you stupid. Sometimes people show you what they think you want to see. They fool you. They don't show their true colors until it's too late."

"No, Mom, you don't understand..."

Mom tilts up my chin, forcing me to look at her. "I understand."

My eyes search hers in confusion.

"I understand, Forrest," she repeats.

Suddenly, her words don't sound like a platitude. There's too much conviction in her voice. I search her eyes for some explanation.

But I'm not ready for the one she gives me:

"The man who got me pregnant with Brian... Forrest, he raped me."

twenty-five

My jaw drops.

"I didn't want you to know, honey. I didn't want either of you to know."

My head spins. "What ... how ... what happened?"

Mom takes a deep breath, exhaling through an O-shaped mouth. "I was in college, walking home from the library one night, back to my dorm. I say night ... it was really just evening ... dusk. It was fall and the days had started getting shorter, so I miscalculated how much time I had to get back to the dorm. Not that walking in the dark should be a problem. Still, you hold every detail under a microscope after the fact, wonder what you did wrong, what you could have done differently ... "

Her eyes skitter away, peering past me. I tilt my head to regain eye contact. "And then what happened?"

She presses her lips together. "I was walking ... and even

though it was dark, there were people around. You know, people are always milling around on a college campus. I didn't feel unsafe at all. Then he called my name..."

"*He.*"

Mom nods. "I'd seen him around a few times before—a couple of parties, I think we even had a class together—and he'd flirted with me a little, but I never really noticed. I didn't even know his name."

Tears spring into her eyes, and now I'm the one squeezing *her* hand. "I didn't even know his name..." she repeats in a whisper.

She takes another deep breath. "Anyway, *he* knew *mine.* He called me. He was walking on the other side of the street, and he called my name. He was standing under a streetlight. He looked so... I don't know... so safe and wholesome, so normal. I waved, said hi, kept walking. Then he crossed the street and started walking with me."

My pulse quickens.

"But even then, I didn't think a thing about it, you know? Just a guy walking across campus with me... stupid, really..."

"It wasn't stupid," I tell her. "You weren't doing anything wrong."

"I really wasn't," Mom says, almost like she's trying to convince herself more than me. "I was just walking home from the library..."

"Then...?"

Mom swallows. "He was nice at first—friendly, casual. I thought he was about to ask me out. And you know what? I probably would have said yes. I was thinking, *He's nice, he's cute... sure, why not?*"

She laughs ruefully.

"I was so naive, Forrest. I'd dated a bit, but nothing serious. I assumed if a guy acted nice, he *was* nice. I didn't distrust a soul in the world... didn't have any reason to."

I nod. I can relate.

"I was much more naive than you are," Mom continues, and now *I'm* the one laughing ruefully.

"You have got to be kidding," I say.

"I mean it," Mom says earnestly. "I know you haven't really dated, but you're so smart, so feisty and savvy... like your dad."

Like my dad. For some reason, I'm incredibly comforted to hear those words.

"I'd been so sheltered all my life," Mom continues. "The same thing you and Brian accuse me of doing to you... sheltering you, smothering you, trying to keep you safe. But as great as you two turned out, I must have done *something* right. Right?"

We share wistful smiles.

"Anyway," Mom says, "before I knew it, the guy was pulling me behind some bushes." She knits her fingers together and rubs them anxiously. "He... he took advantage of me right there in the middle of campus. I could actually hear people nearby, but somehow I couldn't make myself scream. I guess I thought, *Is this really happening?* I just remember feeling so ashamed, so embarrassed..."

I touch her arm. "I'm so sorry, Mom."

The waves lap outside as the moment lingers. "You know what he told me afterward?" Mom says, a bitter edge in her voice. "He said, 'Go clean yourself up.' *Clean yourself up.*"

She studies my face and asks, "Wasn't that a cruel thing to say?"

I try to answer but my throat catches, so I just nod.

"What happened next?" I ask when my voice steadies.

She shrugs. "I went back to my dorm, took a shower, and tried to forget it ever happened."

My eyebrows arch. "You didn't tell anybody?"

Her eyes fall. "Like I told you, sweetie, I was so ashamed. And I couldn't talk to my mother about...about sex. She drilled it into my head to be a good girl, and that was the extent of my sex education. I honestly didn't know if what had just happened was normal or not...like, this is how some girls have their first experiences, maybe? Isn't that insane?"

I avert my eyes. "Before Scott got me alone," I tell her softly, "I could've gotten help. But I was afraid to make a scene. I didn't want to look foolish."

Mom nods. "I didn't want to look foolish either. Or slutty. That was looming large in my head. And how could I have proven it wasn't consensual? I was naive, but I wasn't stupid. I had friends who had casual sex, and it was no big deal for people to make out in the bushes. If I told people I'd just been raped by somebody they saw in their classes, that they knew from fraternity parties...I just couldn't risk feeling the sting of their judgment on top of everything else. It was all I could do to make it through the next day...then the day after that."

I bite my lower lip. "So you just...you just resumed your normal routine?"

She nods with a faraway look in her eye. "That's what I did. I even studied that night, after I showered. I had a test the next day. It sounds ridiculous now, but in retrospect, I'm almost glad I had a test. It was something I had some control over, something I could focus on that made sense. And I got up the next morning, took my test, and went about my life."

I feel a thud in my stomach. "Until you found out..."

"Mmmmmm," Mom says. "Until I found out I was pregnant."

"How long until you knew?"

Mom shrugs. "Way longer than it should have been. Like I said, I was hopelessly naive. I knew my period was late, but I didn't know about any other symptoms, and my menstrual cycle was always kind of erratic anyway, so..."

My heart feels like it will burst, imagining how Mom's world must have imploded as she finally realized what was going on.

"It was my roommate who told me I should take a pregnancy test," Mom says, absently biting the fingernail of her pinkie. "I'm still not sure how she suspected. God knows I never said anything to her."

"So you took a test...?"

Mom nods wearily. "I took a test in the hall bathroom of the dorm. I can still remember the smell of the disinfectant, the voices of girls chatting in other stalls, the swish of the housekeeper's mop on the floor ... anyway, I saw the stick turn blue, then hurried off to my class."

I shake my head. "*Mom ...*"

"I know. I just couldn't absorb it, you know? Of course, I couldn't wish it away for long. At this point, I *had* to deal with reality. I went home that weekend and told my mother. I hardly remember any details at all; the whole thing is just a blur. I don't remember crying much ... just begging my mother not to hate me."

"*Mom,*" I repeat sadly.

"Don't judge Grandma," Mom says. "I don't want you to think she was some ogre I couldn't talk to. It was *my* hang-up, not hers, that it was so hard to confide in her."

Right. I love Grandma, but I know her too well to buy that.

"And she reacted ... well, she reacted as well as could be expected," Mom says in the prim demeanor she always adopts when talking about her parents. "She said she'd handle telling my father, and she'd arrange a doctor's appointment, and we could look into adoption ..."

Her chin quivers and a tear trickles down her cheek. "Adoption," she says. "I guess that brings us full circle."

The waves are crashing onto the beach now, the tide inexorably moving in. "But you *didn't* put him up for adoption," I say in barely a whisper.

Mom smiles through her tears. "I barely knew a single thing at that point in my life," she says. "But I knew I loved my baby. I loved him with all my heart. The only thing that outweighed my need for my parents' approval was my need to protect my baby. I'd have done anything for him. Anything."

"Even ... even knowing how he was conceived?"

Mom gives a sharp nod. "*Especially* knowing how he was conceived. How *dare* that monster make my precious baby's life begin in violence? I vowed my baby would never know another day of violence in his life, would never know anything but love and tenderness. I can't explain it, the depth of love I felt for him. I didn't know it was possible to feel that strongly about another human being, to feel that *connected*."

She smiles at me. "It's the same way I felt with you."

"So when ... when did Dad come into the picture?"

Mom strokes my hair. "I don't ever want you to think I used your father," she says. "It's just ... we'd been friends for a while, and we'd actually gone out a couple of times after the ... after the attack, before I found out I was pregnant. I tried to break things off with him when I realized I was having a baby, but he insisted on seeing me, on talking to me and finding out what was going on. I'd cancelled a date with him, but he came over anyway, came to my dorm room with a handful of wildflowers and said he didn't mind being stood up, but he couldn't stand knowing I was sad without knowing why.

"I told him the whole thing," Mom continues. "I told him about the attack, about how I'd spent the next three months pretending nothing had happened, about how I'd found out I was pregnant in the hall bathroom, how I'd just told my parents and was trying to figure out my next steps, but knowing with every fiber in my being that I would never, ever, *ever* be parted from my baby."

"And he ... proposed?" I say.

Mom laughs lightly. "Actually, yes. It sounds crazy in retrospect, but he really did propose right there on the spot. I didn't say yes right away, but I loved him for asking. It wasn't long before I just *loved* him."

Her eyes are sparkling.

"I wouldn't say it's the most auspicious way to begin a marriage," she continues, "but eighteen years and counting ... that's something, right? I mean, we must be doing something right."

We both jump as we hear pounding on the front door, followed by a low mumble of voices.

Mom and I lock eyes, seeming to mourn the fact that the bubble we've created is about to burst.

We start to walk toward my door, but Mom pulls me back. "I know this is hard," she says, "but we've got to stop him."

I open my mouth to protest again, but she's already moving past me, opening the bedroom door to join the others in the foyer.

Before I join them, I take one last look around my room. Is this really the same room I woke up in twelve hours ago? I feel like I've lived five lifetimes since then.

I take a deep breath and walk into the foyer.

twenty-six

"Ma'am."

Two officers, a man and a woman, nod toward me but avert their eyes. Why can't they look at me? *I* haven't done anything wrong.

"Forrest, this is Officer Thompson and Officer Hull," Dad says, waving in their direction. The man's eyes are still averted, but the woman is sneaking sympathetic glances at me. Have I contracted leprosy in the past half hour?

The man's walkie-talkie beeps and he exchanges a few words with a colleague.

"Ma'am," the female officer asks, "do you mind if I dab a cotton swab on your lip? The part that's bleeding?"

Bleeding. I'm bleeding?

"Sure," I say numbly, but then unexpectedly flinch as she approaches me. Why am I flinching? I've never flinched before when someone walked toward me. Will I be flinching the rest of my life?

The officer halts abruptly, apologetically, then eases slowly closer, her eyes soft and kind. She hesitates a second, then touches the swab to my mouth and drops it into a baggie.

The male officer clears his throat. "Do you have any injuries other than the ones we can see? The cut on your lip and the bruises on your arm?"

My arms are bruised? Oh.

My head swims as I try to process the question, then I shake my head.

The female officer asks, "Mind if I get some pictures?"

"Um..."

Mom and Dad physically steady me as she retrieves a camera from her pocket, taking close-ups of my arms. I glance at them and notice the angry purple welts forming where Scott's fingers dug into my flesh. I shiver.

Next, the officer photographs my bottom lip, the outside first, then shots of the inside as I pull it down for the lens. Only now do I realize that I taste blood. My mouth suddenly feels foreign to me—puffy and alien and ugly and shocking. How dare that asshole make my own body feel repulsive to me.

The officers exchange glances and the man says, "May I ask you to step into the other room and change your clothes? As carefully as possible, please. Then put them into this bag."

He hands the bag to Mom and says to her, "If you note any injuries on your daughter other than the ones we can see, please let us know immediately. We'll take her to an emergency room, where she can be checked thoroughly in total privacy."

"I'm fine," I snap, wondering how it's possible to be "checked thoroughly" by a stranger, any stranger, in "total privacy." I know these police officers are just doing their job, but I feel like a lab specimen. Will my body ever feel like my own again?

"And why do you need my clothes?" I ask.

"Evidence," the officer explains softly.

"What evidence?" I ask, then start looking at my clothes more closely. "He didn't rip them or anything, did he?"

"No, ma'am," he says. "But DNA, hair . . . you'd be surprised how much evidence a perp leaves behind."

A perp? DNA? What parallel universe have I stumbled into?

Mom guides me back into my bedroom and closes the door behind us, then gently lifts my shirt over my head. I hand her my shorts and panties, too dazed to feel modest. She drops them all into the bag, then helps me into fresh underwear and a robe.

We walk back out. Dad and the officers have settled into seats in the family room, Dad on the couch. He jumps up when he sees me, then guides Mom and me to sit beside him.

"Ma'am, I need to record this conversation, if that's okay," the male officer says. I nod, and he asks, "Can you give me a description of the man who attacked you?"

My hands fumble. "Um…" I mutter a few words: "young," "tanned," "sandy-blond hair"…

"Eye color?" he asks.

I dunno… gray? Brown? Blue? "I've only seen him, like, four times," I say, pressing a nail against my mouth, then yanking it away as I feel my bottom lip sting.

The officer pulls out his walkie-talkie and relays the information to his colleague, who I presume is combing the beach right now in search of a guy who fits the description of probably five-hundred other guys within a ten-mile radius.

"What's the point?" I groan. "Surely he's long gone by now."

The officer puts the walkie-talkie back on his belt loop. "You say his name is Scott?"

I nod. "That's what he told me. I don't know his last name. He told me he's been staying with his aunt this summer in her beach house… that he just finished painting her bathroom or something…"

Suspicion flickers in the officer's eyes.

"That should help narrow him down," Dad says.

The officer shrugs. "Lots of locals hang out on the beach and tell girls they're staying in one of the beach houses… trying to impress them, I guess. I know the people on this street pretty well, and I don't know of any who have a nephew staying with them this summer…"

"You wouldn't necessarily know that," Mom counters.

He nods. "Yes, ma'am. But lots of folks keep us posted about their guests, especially guests staying a long while, so that we'll know who to look out for. Of course, we'll look into it."

"Why?" I mutter. "What's the point? It'll just be his word against mine."

"The point is to get a rapist off the streets," Dad says.

I start crying, and Dad wraps me in his arms. "It's okay, sweetie…it's okay…"

But nothing feels okay. I wonder if anything will ever feel okay again.

twenty-seven

Mom hands me a cup of tea.

"Careful," she says as I take it. "It's hot."

I sip it as Dad smooths my hair. We've been sitting on the couch since the officers left. How long has that been? Five minutes? Fifteen? An hour? I truly have no idea.

Mom closes the curtains with brisk efficiency. I don't think those curtains have ever been closed before; who blocks a view of the ocean? But I'm grateful for the gesture. Any extra layer of protection, any way to minimize my exposure to the world, feels insanely comforting. Will I ever be able to enjoy looking out a window again, even with an ocean for a backdrop? *Damn* Scott for making the world suddenly seem so sinister.

"I'm so sorry this happened to you," Dad says.

I turn toward him and squeeze his hand to steady my shaking. "I never want to see him again. I don't want to have to talk about this with anybody. True, I wouldn't want another girl to go through this, but how many other girls would be as stupid as ... "

"*You're not stupid,*" Dad insists. "He's an animal, and he deserves to—"

"He won't get caught anyway," I say in a flat voice. "'Sandy-blond hair.'" I snort, disgusted at myself, then quip, "Anything else I can do for you, Officer?"

"But you'd be able to identify him in a lineup," Dad says.

I squeeze my eyes shut and shake my head. "I just want to pretend it never happened."

Mom sits beside me and pats my hand. "Things don't work that way," she says.

Dad rubs my hair some more. "I'm so sorry all of this has hit you at once," he says. "I'm so sorry I couldn't protect you."

Then he sniffles.

Oh my god. My dad is crying. I think I can handle anything in the world except this.

I put my tea on the coffee table and wrap my arms around his neck. "Don't cry, Daddy."

Mom rubs my back while he and I weep into each other's necks for a few moments, our hiccupped breaths pulsing lightly against each other's chests.

When I pull away, we lock tearstained eyes and I say, "I'm sorry I was such a brat when you were trying to tell me about ... about how you and Mom got together. Mom explained it, and I just want you to know ... you're my hero."

Dad manages a weak smile. "Are you kidding? My family is the best thing that ever happened to me. I'm no hero. I hit the jackpot."

"I'm sorry I didn't understand ... "

"It's okay, honey, it's okay. I'm glad your mom was the one to fill in the gaps. That's the way it should have been."

Dad hugs me again, and Mom wraps her arms around both of us.

I've never loved them so much in my life.

twenty-eight

"Let's get one thing straight."

Mom, Dad, and I glance anxiously at the foyer. In the two hours that have passed since Brian ferried Olivia and her psycho mom out of the house, the planet has flipped off its axis. They just don't know it yet.

Brian doesn't even have time to shut the door before the lunatic lady is railing at us again, hand on hip.

"Nobody's arranging any bait-and-switch adoption with my grandchild," Olivia's mother says, spitting out every word.

Mom squeezes her eyes shut. We get up from the couch and join them in the foyer.

"I've *told* you that," Olivia groans. "Brian's mother wasn't trying to do anything sneaky or underhanded. She was just exploring our options—"

"I'll tell you your *options*," her mother says.

"—and once she realized we wouldn't even consider

adoption," Olivia continues, gritting her teeth, "the case was closed. This is a non-issue, Mom."

"It didn't sound like a non-issue when you were sobbing to me on the phone yesterday!"

Olivia tosses a hand in the air. "Have you listened to a word I said?"

"I'm not interested in *your* words, I'm interested in *her* actions!" her mother says, flinging a dagger-like finger in Mom's direction. Then she faces Mom, her eyes ablaze, as she whips a lock of long blonde hair off her shoulder. "You may call all the shots in *your* family, but you don't call them in *mine!*"

Olivia shakes her head miserably, fighting back tears. "Am I in your family now, Mom?"

The woman spins on a heel and faces her daughter. "What's that supposed to mean?"

Olivia struggles to look at her, but her eyes fall short. "I never felt like I was in your family."

"Oh, *please.*"

Dad holds up his palm. "Look. It's getting late. Nobody is putting anybody's baby up for adoption. Brian and Olivia made it clear that they want to raise their child, and, of course, the choice is theirs. *Theirs alone.* There's no point in rehashing a discussion that's already been settled."

"I don't trust her," Olivia's mother says, pointing at Mom again. "She'll do something behind our backs, just like she concocted this adoption thing behind our backs. She thinks she can walk all over my daughter. She thinks I'm some trailer trash she doesn't have to deal with. Well, guess what: *you're dealing with me* whether you like it or not!"

Mom's patient but contemptuous expression makes it pretty clear she actually *doesn't* like it but is grudgingly resigned to the fact.

"And since it *is* getting late," Dad says, stubbornly picking up where he left off, "I suggest we all get a good night's sleep and continue this discussion in the morning, when we're all feeling calmer."

"I drove six hours to get here," Olivia's mother whines.

"You can spend the night with us," Brian says, ignoring Mom's ensuing flash of indignation. He looks at me. "Forrest, would you mind sleeping on the couch?"

Mom puts her arm around me and presses me close before I can respond. "Forrest is sleeping with *me* tonight," she informs the group.

Dad nods gamely. "So I guess *I'm* sleeping on the couch."

"I can, Dad," Brian offers. "You can have my bed."

Olivia pipes up weakly, "No, my mom can sleep in a—"

"Oh, for heaven's sake," Mom mutters. "Let's all just go to bed."

Brian nods, then gives me a double take. "What's wrong with *you?*" he asks.

I wrap my arms together and shiver.

"Your mouth's bleeding," Brian persists. "Did you fall?"

Mom shakes her head and mouths "*later*" to him. Then she takes my hand and leads me toward the master bedroom before firing a parting shot at Olivia's mother: "I trust you can make yourself comfortable."

––––––––––

"...and then the ice cream was shooting out of my nostrils."

I giggle uncontrollably.

Mom and I have lain in bed all night talking, and at some point our Earnest Conversation degenerated into full-blown giddiness.

Mom tries halfheartedly to shush me, but she's giggling too.

"We've never done this before," I say wistfully when our laughter dies down. "Just hung out and been silly together."

Mom's jaw drops in mock indignation. "Are you forgetting Tipsy the Tootsie Thief?"

I explode into a new round of giggles. When I was little, Mom would wake me up in the morning pretending to be Tipsy the Tootsie Thief, sneaking in to steal my toes. I always wear socks to bed (weird, I know), and Tipsy's job was to snatch a sock off my foot and grab as many toes as she could wrangle, one by one, which made me squeal with laughter, howling as I tried to retrieve my sock while individual toes were tickled and "plucked" from my foot.

"*Tipsy*," I say now. "What kind of name is that for a kiddie game? Tipsy means drunk, Mom."

"Oh for heaven's sake," she huffs playfully.

And truly, I didn't know what tipsy meant until, like,

middle school. Mom's right...she protected Brian and me with the ferocity of a Fort Knox guard, so I was always approximately a zillion times more naive than my friends and classmates. Mom and Dad never had more than an occasional glass of wine, so my only association with "tipsy" growing up was "tootsie thief." God knows it's been annoying as hell, being treated like a hothouse flower while my worldlier friends were explaining the intricacies of French kissing to me during sixth-grade gym class, but I kinda love Mom for it right this moment. I'm sure lots of sacrifices were involved to raise spectacularly clueless kids. Mom rose to that challenge like a prize fighter.

Her overprotectiveness was grating enough by adolescence to make me spurn tootsie thieves and other lame stabs at silliness, so the kid stuff fell by the wayside. Curled lips and eye rolls moved in to fill the void. I know, I know, that's what teenagers do, but my stomach tightens a little with the sudden realization that my snottiness must be hard on Mom.

So it feels good to be silly with her, even at four o'clock in the morning. It's nice to shake off the intensity of the past few hours. We've tackled some pretty tough topics, and we've debriefed about our ever-evolving feelings toward Olivia.

But as much as I'm enjoying the giddiness that's slipped in through the cracks, there's one more Earnest Topic I need to broach. I pull the down-filled comforter tighter under my chin.

"So," I say, "Brian knew, and I didn't. What's up with that?"

Mom's eyes skitter away. "I didn't want *either* of you to know," she says softly. "I wanted to create a perfect, complication-free world for you both."

"So ... how did he end up finding out?"

Mom purses her lips. "Your father insisted. He'd wanted to be honest with both of you from the beginning. Well ... as honest as you can be about something like that. He said secrets always have a way of spilling out, and that you both deserved to know, and it would be easier if ... "

She clears her throat. "Anyway. He was right, of course. But I fought him every step of the way. How do you tell a precious little boy that the man raising him, his *hero*, isn't really his father? And besides, misleading him didn't even seem like a lie. Your father *is* his father. Brian's more like Dad than you are!"

"So ... when did he tell him?"

Mom sighs deeply. "Right around his birthday. Dad always said age eighteen was the latest he would postpone telling him. He knew how hard it would be for Brian, but he said Brian would never trust us again if he found out from someone other than us, and he wouldn't let him start his adulthood with this albatross hanging around his neck."

"His birthday ... " I say to myself. "Last summer ... when he started dating Olivia ... when he started breaking out in rashes .... "

Mom nods, her eyes pained.

"I said to your dad, 'See? Still think it was such a great

idea?' I'd have given anything if we could all have just gone to our graves without—"

"A few rashes, but that was it," I say, still talking to myself. "I mean, it's amazing Brian was so strong about it. He never said a word to me."

"He wanted to protect you," Mom says. "We all did."

"So at a time when his whole world explodes into a million pieces, *he's* worried about protecting *me*."

Mom smiles. "That's our Brian. Like I said: just like Dad."

I take a deep breath. It all seems so clear now. I *knew* something was off with Brian, I *knew* it. I blamed it all on Olivia, and god knows she was a handy target at the time, but this buzz of anxiety has haunted me for months now: *Something's wrong with my brother. Something's wrong with my brother.* Yes. It all makes sense now.

"Was anyone ever going to tell me?" I ask Mom. "Not that it wasn't a total delight to have Olivia's mother tip me off."

Mom touches my forehead with cool fingertips. "I hate that she did that. That *woman*, who couldn't even be bothered to raise her own child, coming into *my* home and shaking up *my baby's* world..."

My eyes fall. "Like Dad said: secrets always end up spilling out."

"Still," Mom says. "I think we could have made it to the finish line with you."

I laugh in spite of myself. "Any other secrets you were planning on taking to the finish line?"

Mom raises an eyebrow. "No, that one pretty much consumed all my energy. Well ... there *was* that one time when I told you Grandma was sick so I could avoid having you go to the mountains for the weekend with Gina Preswell's family. I'd always heard her mother had a drinking problem ... "

"And the time you told me we were buying a piano to rope me into piano lessons!"

We both start giggling again, sputtering into our fingertips.

"You are such a control freak!" I say, still laughing.

"Oh, *you* try making it through motherhood without an occasional white lie to grease the wheels," she says.

I stick my tongue out at her and she narrows her eyes, and we start giggling again.

I gaze into space. "Think Brian and Olivia have a shot at this family thing?"

Mom sighs. "I guess we'll find out. She's a nice girl ... she's just so young ... "

"Not much younger than you were when you got pregnant," I observe, glancing at her quickly for a post-facto sensitivity check.

"Exactly," Mom says quietly. "I know too much. Even with your father in the picture, it wasn't easy. I know their intentions are good, and heaven knows Brian will be a wonderful father. But Olivia, growing up without a mother ... I do worry."

"Maybe it'll make her a *better* mother than she would have been otherwise," I muse. "I mean, nobody understands a mother's importance better than someone who hasn't had one."

"Mmm," Mom says noncommittally.

"Mom," I say firmly, "you gotta give them a chance."

Mom waves her arm expansively around the bedroom. "Uh, hello, she's spending the summer *in our home*. Does that qualify as a chance?"

"Not if you're plotting behind her back."

"Oh, enough with the 'plotting'! Everybody's making me sound like Mata Hari for having the common sense to explore a couple of options."

"I have no idea who Mata Hari is."

"Well ... you should read more."

"Yeah, *that's* my problem: I don't read enough."

We start giggling again.

"I think Olivia's gonna be a good mom," I say after a moment. "And of course it goes without saying that I'm going to be a spectacular aunt."

Mom taps her fingers together lightly. "Ready or not ..."

twenty-nine

I rub my eyes, squint at the clock, then gasp and jump out of bed.

One fifteen? *In the afternoon?* Have I really slept half the day away?

Yes. Bright midday sun is peeking through the closed bedroom blinds and voices waft from the family room. After a couple of minutes, I hear Olivia and her wackadoodle mother say goodbye, shutting the front door behind them.

I get out of bed, strum my hand through my bedhead, brush my teeth with my finger in the master bedroom, pull on a pair of shorts and a T-shirt, and walk into the family room.

Mom is in the kitchen, singing cheerfully despite the fact that she probably only got about ninety minutes of sleep last night. Dad and Brian are watching baseball.

They smile when I walk in. "Hi, Yogi," Dad says.

I flash a peace sign and ask, "Where'd Olivia and Cruella go?"

"Lunch," Dad says. "Her mom is headed back home from there."

Brian jumps up from his seat. "Sit here, sit here," he tells me.

I look at Dad and groan. "He knows."

Dad shrugs apologetically.

"I just want you to get comfortable," Brian says.

"It's okay, Bri," I say.

He claps his hands together. "Okay then. Wanna take a walk on the beach?"

"I'm okay," I repeat softly. "Really."

"I know," Brian says, rubbing a hand through his hair. "I just feel like walking on the beach." He eyes me warily. "Okay with you?"

I sigh. "Sure."

He and I walk out the back door, across the deck, and down the stairs. I take a deep breath. It's okay ... *I'm safe now.*

As we head toward the ocean, I say, "So ... anything interesting happen in *your* life lately?"

Brian laughs lightly and kicks the surf with his bare foot.

"I dunno ... things have been pretty slow. I might have to take up bungee jumping."

We keep walking.

"I'm so pissed that jerk put his hands on you," Brian finally says in a brittle voice. Like Dad, he tries his hardest to sound casual when he's least inclined to be casual.

"It's okay. I'm fine."

Brian smacks a fist into his open palm. "If the police don't find him, I will. I swear to god, if it's the last thing I do, I'll—"

"Chill, okay?"

We walk in silence for a couple of moments, occasionally making way for a hurtling toddler or a doddering old couple all done up in floral prints and floppy hats.

"So," Brian says when our path is clear again for the foreseeable future. "I hear the big family secret is out of the bag."

Again with the casual.

My first instinct is to make a wisecrack, but the remark gets stuck in my throat. Brian reaches over and takes my hand, squeezing it gently. He's still looking straight ahead, still loping along, still committed to casual. But I'm so touched by the gesture that I impulsively stop in my tracks and hug him.

And he lets me. He even hugs me back. We listen to each other swallow hard.

"You should have told me," I finally whisper when I trust my voice not to crack.

"Nah," he says as we pull apart. "That would have messed up my master plan: getting Olivia pregnant and having her crazy mother show up on our doorstep to let the cat out of the bag. That was definitely the way to go. Just took a little planning and patience on my part."

I laugh and he laughs back. It feels so good to laugh.

We resume our walk, our forearms brushing lightly

together. Twinkly beads of sunlight glisten on the breaking waves.

"What was it like?" I ask Brian. "Hearing the news... what was that like?"

In my peripheral vision, I see him shrug. "Kinda sucked," he says. "Can't say I saw it coming. It was near my birthday— right before or right after—and I thought Dad was about to launch into some kind of 'Son, you're a man now' speech. Either that or a 'By the way, have I mentioned lately that drugs are bad?' speech."

I laugh lightly at his totally-bogus-baritone Dad impression.

"So... what *did* Dad say?"

Brian shrugs again. "Just... 'Son, you know how much I love you, but I think there's something you should know...'"

Slosh, slosh, slosh go our footsteps through the waves.

"But he never stopped looking me in the eye," Brian adds, a warm breeze blowing against our faces. "That meant a lot to me. I thought, *He's not afraid of this; he's not afraid of us.* It made me feel... not afraid."

I nod, blinking away tears.

Slosh, slosh, slosh.

"What about Mom?" I say. "What did she say after you found out?"

Brian shrugs. "We, like, hugged. She cried. I told her everything was cool. And it was. Life went back to normal after that."

"No it didn't," I say, looking down. "That's when you started breaking out in rashes."

"Oh yeah. Thanks for reminding me, by the way." Brian pauses, then adds, "You know, I never even made that connection."

"It's when you started dating Olivia, too," I say cautiously. "And when you decided to blow off college."

"Forrest, honest to god, I never associated any of those things with 'the news.' I was just living my life."

"But making really weird choices."

"Yeah, dating the prettiest girl in school was way out there."

I jostle him. "You know I'm cool with Olivia now," I say, then giggle as Brian makes an exaggerated gesture of relief. "But college...blowing off college was weird. Was it, like, a way to get back at Mom? Even though it wasn't her fault?"

Brian runs his fingers through his hair. "Nah. Although, frankly, there's never a *bad* occasion to get back at Mom." Pause. "Of course I never blamed her. I hated that bastard for hurting her...like I hate that bastard Scott."

I wince hearing Brian say his name.

"But I guess it did make me rethink my priorities," Brian says. "I felt this new sense of liberty in living for myself, making my own choices instead of trying to please Mom."

I crinkle my eyebrows together. "But what if you'd *liked* college? What if what Mom wanted is really what would have made you the happiest?"

"Uh, in the first place, I'm *going* to college," Brian snaps playfully. "God, you act like Starrett Community College is Alcatraz or something."

"No, no," I protest. "Harvard, Yale, Vanderbilt, Starrett Community College...they all share that Ivy League vibe."

He chuckles. "Yeah, well, a degree is a degree. I'm happy. And I don't break out in rashes anymore. It's all good, right?"

I smile.

Slosh, slosh, slosh.

"Do you ever think about *him*?" I ask. "Are you ever curious about—"

"No."

That's it. Just no.

I stop abruptly.

Brian turns and looks at me, then follows my gaze. Some guys are playing Frisbee a few yards up the beach.

My heart pounds through my shirt.

"That's them."

thirty

Brian thrusts out his chest.

"Scott?" he asks me, his voice eerily calm.

"No," I say, panting softly, "he's not there. But those are the guys I've seen him playing Frisbee with."

Brian starts running toward them. I freeze for a nano-second, then trot to catch up with him.

"Brian, wait..."

Brian lunges toward one of the Frisbee players, stopping only when their noses are practically touching. "Excuse me," he barks. "Looking for a guy named Scott."

The Frisbee player backs away warily and eyes his friends.

"Uh... he's not here," the guy says.

"So tell me where I can find him."

"Brian..." I plead.

"I dunno, man," the Frisbee player says. "He's thrown

a Frisbee around with us a few times, but it's not like we hang out..."

"Just point out where he's staying," Brian says, moving closer again and pumping his fists by his side.

The guy scratches his head. "Where he's *staying*?"

"Yeah. He's staying at his aunt's place, right?"

The guy looks genuinely puzzled, again exchanging glances with his friends.

"I don't think so..." he says.

"Sure he is," Brian says, muscling another step closer. "Just finished painting her bathroom. Show me the house, bro. Just want to know which house is his."

The guy backs away a bit. "Yeah, he painted somebody's bathroom recently, but it wasn't his aunt's. Just some lady on the beach who hired him to do some painting. That's what he told *us*, anyhow. Think he said he finished the job. But he doesn't *live* here... he lives somewhere in town, I think. He just hangs out on the beach a lot. I don't even know his last name."

Brian studies his face, then looks at his friends. "All I want to do is talk to the guy," he says, trying not to sound as menacing as he looks.

"We'd help you if we could," one of the guys says. "But we really don't know him that well. The guy's kind of a jerk, actually."

Brian considers his words.

"I really need to talk to him."

"Yeah," the first guy says. "If we see him again, we'll

definitely tell him you're looking for him. You live on the beach...?"

"*I'll* find *him*," Brian says. "Like I said...just need to talk. So...I'll head this way every so often, see if I get lucky and catch him hanging out with you guys..."

"Yeah, yeah," they murmur, assuring Brian they'll be on the lookout.

Brian stands there for a long moment, studying their faces, one at a time. "Great," he says. "Appreciate it."

———————

"What are you *doing*?"

Brian is walking so fast up the beach, I have to trot to catch up with him.

"Can't let the summer go by without introducing myself to ol' Scott, can I?"

I breathlessly pull on his arm, forcing him to stop. "*Don't!*" I beg. "I can't stand thinking of you breathing the same oxygen as him. And if he has any sense at all, he'll lie low. I'll probably never see him again. And that's all that matters. I just want him to disappear. Please don't make me have to deal with him again, Brian."

Brian's eyes soften. "*You* won't have to deal with him at all."

"I don't want him polluting our lives! In *any* way, in *any* form, on *any*body's terms. *Please* let this all go away."

Brian's chest seems to literally be deflating before my

eyes. He sighs. "Okay," he says grudgingly. "If I run into him, I don't make any promises, but I'll just...chill. Okay?"

I exhale through puffed-out cheeks. "Thank you."

We start walking again at a normal pace, and after a couple of minutes, my heart stops racing.

I'm safe, I remind myself. *My big brother's here. I'm safe.*

————

"God, Forrest, I am *so sorry*."

"You'll have to be more specific."

Olivia smiles, but her eyes are sad. "I'm sorry about everything. But mostly about...about your parents...about the secret."

I guess Olivia has been waiting for me in our bedroom. She was out with her mom all afternoon, so we haven't had a chance to talk about...about...well, about any of the Jerry Springer issues that have come crashing into my life in the past twenty-four hours.

I'm toweling my hair dry from the shower as I walk to the dresser in my robe.

"I shoulda hooked up with your mom eons ago," I muse. "Gotta hand it to her, she can cough up family secrets like nobody's business."

"I'm *so sorry*," Olivia repeats. "It was so stupid of me to tell her."

I turn to look at her. "It's okay. Really. It's okay."

Tears fill Olivia's eyes. "And Scott...oh, Forrest, it's just so *awful*."

I walk over to her. "Thanks for the things you said to me...for watching out for me, for trying to—"

"I didn't do anything," Olivia moans. "I should have done so much more. I should have stayed with you on the beach and made sure he couldn't come near you...I mean, I just thought he was a *player*, which is bad enough. I didn't know he was—"

"It's okay," I say in barely a whisper. "*I'm* okay. I handled it. And now...well, I'm a lot wiser now."

Olivia shakes her head, her eyes still teary. "Not all guys are like that," she insists. "I had some bad experiences with guys before I met Brian. I mean, they're out there...the guys who just want to use you...but they're not *all* that way, Forrest."

She hugs me spontaneously, and I hug her back for a long moment.

As our arms untangle, I say, "So your mom headed back home?"

Olivia nods.

"I miss her already," I say.

Olivia giggles through her tears. "I hate her," she says. "*Hate* her, *hate* her, *hate* her."

She plops on the floor and leans against the bottom bunk. I sit next to her.

"You know what's pathetic?" she says wistfully. "No matter how many times she lets me down, I always come back for more. I always crave her approval, always hope the next time will be different, always carve out whatever little slice of my soul I think I can toss at her to keep her coming back."

"You're better than her," I say, and I mean it.

Olivia nods. "She set the bar pretty low."

We giggle again.

"But I'm gonna be a great mom," Olivia says with a look of steely determination. "Whatever my mom would do, I'll do the opposite."

"Excellent plan."

She looks into space. "Do you think Brian started dating me just because he was so vulnerable? That if he hadn't found out about his dad, we'd never have gotten together?"

I shake my head. "Nope. I think he loves you."

I mean it.

Olivia considers my words. "I couldn't believe that at first. I thought, *He's such a great guy; what could he possibly see in me?*"

I look at her and raise an eyebrow. "Uh, *hello*," I say.

She blushes. "I mean it. I think when your own mom bails on you ... well ... it really does a number on your self-esteem."

I feel a pinch in my heart. How *dare* Olivia base her self-esteem on her mother's selfishness. How *dare* her stupid mother create that destiny for her.

Dad's words echo in my head: *Don't judge people by their parents.* I love my dad for saying that. I love him for *living* it.

My fingers dangle over my knees. "Do you think if

your mom had stuck around," I ask, "that you'd be in a different place now?"

She shrugs, both of us still gazing into space. "I wish she'd stuck around. But I wouldn't want to be in a different place."

A moment passes. "It's weird how my parents ended up together," I say, "but it seems to have worked out okay."

Olivia's eyes turn wistful. "I'm beginning to think that most people just kind of *fall* into adulthood. You know, when you're little, you think of your future like a buffet—I can have this, or this, or that, or a little bit of everything—and when you grow up, you realize you're more like a kid at a parade, waiting for a clown to toss some candy your way, then hoping you can beat out the other kids to grab a piece, then realizing you're stuck with whatever ends up in your hand. But happy to have it."

I nod. "Deep. I guess the secret is being happy to have it."

"Well, it is candy."

I shrug in agreement, then say, "What if, instead of throwing you candy, the clown runs over your foot with his unicycle?"

Olivia *mmmmm*s in contemplation. "Then you're screwed."

The fan whirs overhead.

"So you're gonna do surveillance on all the guys I hang around in the future?" I ask her playfully.

"Well, I *do* have a lot of experience in these areas," she says. "Maybe I can be your go-to girl when it comes to guys. And you can be my go-to girl when it comes to ... "

"Vocabulary?" I suggest after an excruciatingly long pause.

"Yeah. Vocabulary."

"Then I guess we've got each other's backs."

thirty-one

"It'll only take a few minutes, honey."

My nails dig into my palms. "Olivia and I were just headed out for yogurt," I tell Dad.

Olivia touches my hand. "We'll come with you." She glances at Brian. "We'll all come."

A week has passed since Scott attacked me. The knot in my stomach hasn't yet loosened, but my lip has healed, and the bruises on my arm have faded to light pink. I've trained my brain not to look at my arms; I'm nauseated by the outline of his fingers. Yes, I've gotten pretty good at closing that door in my mind. Sometimes, five whole minutes pass without me thinking about that night.

But I've overheard hushed phone conversations between my parents and the police, so I know I can't wish the experience away.

In a way, I'd give anything to confront Scott, to scream

at him and throw my pain at his feet. But I think of his soulless eyes and shiver. He doesn't give a shit about my pain. And I truly don't want to devote another nanosecond of my life to thinking about him.

But other girls are out there...

I take a deep breath. "Okay," I tell Dad. "Let's go."

The five of us file into the car and head for the police station. All these years I've spent my summers here, and who knew where the police station was? It seems as jolting to think about a police station at the beach as it does to think about the sewage system at an amusement park. But on this gorgeous summer day, the police station is where we are heading.

In the car, Mom and Dad tell me in murmured voices what to expect: people have been questioned, statements have been filed, evidence has been gathered—and now a lineup of guys is awaiting me at the station behind a one-way mirror. Scott will never lay eyes on me; we won't exchange a single word of conversation. I just have to look at the guys and point out which one is Scott. Then leave. That's it.

So why do I feel like I'm going to throw up? Olivia squeezes my hand in the back seat, and Brian tosses his arm around my neck.

I keep my eyes on the sea of fuchsia crepe myrtle blooming in islands in the middle of the street. Spackle Beach... such a beautiful place.

I correct myself. *Sparkle* Beach.

Our family isn't spackling over things anymore.

I swallow hard.

It'll be okay.

I clench my sweaty palms.

"You're sure he can't see me?"

The officer nods. "I guarantee it, ma'am."

My family is waiting outside while the officer and I sit behind the glass. The five guys standing in front of me all have similar features, but one face—the fourth one—is unmistakable. I'd know that asshole anywhere.

"He looks like he's staring at me," I tell the officer, who nods and assures me he hears that a lot.

But there's more to it than that. Yes, Scott's eyes are still soulless, but his gaze is smug and cocky. He holds his head high and throws his shoulders back. His good looks, his confidence, his swagger... they've clearly served him well in the past. And he seems to instinctively know where to level his eyes. Even though he can't see me, he knows I'm on the other side. His gaze is a clearly a dare, a challenge, a threat: *Bring it, bitch.*

But rather than cowering, I stand taller. Yes, he's a sociopath, but he's just a guy... a pathetic, flesh-and-blood guy who I'm guessing has skated through life without so much as glancing backward at his victims. But I'm not in his past; I'm right here, right in front of him, facing him, and maybe for the first time forcing him to face himself.

I have no delusions; his conscience is probably irredeemably AWOL. But I spoke up, and he's having to deal with me whether he wants to or not. I'm so grateful Mom and Dad insisted that I speak up. I feel twelve feet tall.

"That's him," I say simply. "Blue polo shirt, fourth guy from the left."

This is for you too, Mom, I think, then stand taller still.

The officer searches my eyes. "You're sure?"

I nod. "One hundred percent."

Yes. Twelve feet tall.

thirty-two

"No *way*!"

I squeal and leap into the air before throwing my arms around Shelley.

I was already peering at her mom's car in our driveway, confused at first, wondering what was up, and then . . .

Then I saw Shelley come bounding out my front door, her strawberry-blonde hair blowing in the sea breeze.

Dad grins broadly. "Surprised?" he asks.

But I've already jumped out of the car and swept Shelley into my arms.

"What are you doing here?" I ask her, still squealing. Just for the record, squealing is *so* unlike me.

"My mom drove me," Shelley says. "She's inside."

"She's a rock star," I say, then notice my family beaming as they approach us. This is the first time I've seen Mom and Dad look happy in a week.

Shelley offers hugs all around, then we go inside and join her mom.

I'd waited a few days before telling Shelley about the attempted rape. I wanted to talk to her, and I knew she'd be there for me, but I somehow wanted to keep as much of my world as pure as possible. Maybe if I could contain this filthy stain, then I could ease back into my real life without any seepage.

But then I thought about Olivia, feeling unworthy all those years because her mother ditched her. And I thought about Mom, too ashamed after her rape to tell a single soul, then slogging through the next few weeks feeling utterly alone. She probably never would have told *anyone* if she hadn't gotten pregnant—just carried that horrible secret all her life.

It's not fair to feel shame for something you can't control. Scott carries the filthy stain, not me. So I called Shelley last night and told her everything.

Little did I know that she'd spend the next hour working the phones with my parents to arrange a surprise week-long visit. And now here she is. Mom had left a key under the mat when we left for the police station.

Mom hugs Shelley's mom, then scurries to the kitchen and pulls a huge bowl of fresh fruit and a plastic container of chicken salad out of the fridge.

"I can't stay, Maureen," Shelley's mom is saying from the family room.

"You've got to eat!" Mom says cheerily, and I think, *This is the mom I know.*

In no time, she's set the table and put a vase of fresh flowers in the center. The table seats only six, so Shelley and I squeeze into a chair together, wolf down a few bites, and beg off so we can hit the beach.

The moms offer fluttery waves and tell us to be careful.

"Hey, Liv, you and Bri come too," I say.

They hop up from the table and we duck into the bedrooms to change. Soon we're all emerging in bathing suits, surfboards tucked under our arms.

"See ya," we call as we head to the deck, the surging waves of high tide beckoning.

The sea breeze brushes against my cheek as we run onto the beach. I *can* own all the parts of my life; I know this now. Things can suck one day and be cool the next, and I can claim it all, can absorb it all without feeling defined by any specific circumstances. Brian learned that a year ago. I'm learning it now.

And I've never felt lighter on my feet.

———

"Scythe?" Olivia asks incredulously, pronouncing the *C*.

I laugh lightly. "I promise it's a real word," I say as I tally my Scrabble score.

"This is my last Scrabble game with you," Olivia says, fake pouting. "You and your dad are, like, wordaholics."

"That's not a word," I say, and Liv playfully throws a tile at me.

It's after midnight, and considering we spent hours today on the beach, you'd think we'd be dead to the world right now. But I'm still on a Shelley high, so she and Liv and I are playing Scrabble in the family room.

Well ... kinda playing. We're too punch-drunk for our hearts to be in it, so it's a lot of gabbing interspersed with a smattering of scything.

"I hope my baby's brilliant like you guys," Olivia says, and Shelley sucks in her breath.

Olivia gives me a startled look. "She doesn't know?"

I shrug. "She knows now."

"You're pregnant?" Shelley asks, then squeals when Olivia nods.

Then she casts an indignant look at me. "You didn't tell me?" Shelley says. "I thought I was your BFF!"

"I'm not only brilliant, I'm discreet," I say, collecting more tiles for my next turn.

"Are you and Brian getting married?" Shelley asks.

Olivia smiles and nods. "I know we've got a lot to figure out, but I think we're gonna be just fine."

"Do you know what the rumor was?" Shelley asks her conspiratorially. "That you were bulimic."

I roll my eyes. "You don't tell the people being gossiped about what the gossip is."

But Olivia is giggling. "I've heard that one for two years," she says. "I think I had cancer at one point too. Oh, and I was a drug addict. But bulimia ... that one had legs."

We laugh so hard that Liv starts patting her hand in

the air to shush us. "Everybody's asleep," she reminds us. "Hey, why am I such a gossip magnet, by the way?"

"Because you're drop-dead beautiful," Shelley answers matter-of-factly.

"Then why aren't you and I gossip magnets?" I ask Shelley, and we explode into a fresh burst of laughter.

"You two *are* drop-dead beautiful," Liv assures us. "But you gotta get that whole diva vibe going. *That's* what cranks up the rumor mill, I think."

"Oooohh, will you teach us?" Shelley asks, folding her hands under her chin.

"I'd teach you, but then I'd have to kill you."

Shelley smiles. "Who knew you were so cool?" she asks Olivia.

I smile.

My sentiments exactly: *Who knew?*

thirty-three

"I'm not saying it's hopeless."

Mom, Dad, and I cast anxious glances around our kitchen table. Two more weeks have passed; we'll be heading home on Sunday. We'd heard that Scott was out on bail, but until this meeting with the assistant district attorney, the details had been sketchy.

"Our best bet may be getting him to plead down to sexual assault," the lawyer continues, her voice crisp with brisk efficiency.

"What's the difference between attempted rape and sexual assault?" Mom asks her.

She frowns. "About twenty years."

"No!" Mom says. "I'm sorry, Ms. Pickett, I'm not trying to tell you how to do your job, but I can't stand the thought of Scott getting a slap on the wrist. The thought of him doing this to someone else..."

Ms. Pickett leans into the table. "*His* story," she says, "is that Forrest invented the rape charge because she was mad he'd stood her up that night."

I guffaw indignantly.

"He hurt her!" Mom responds. "They have pictures... evidence..."

"And that's good," Ms. Pickett continues, "but he said Forrest told him she 'liked it rough.'" She looks at me apologetically. "He said he has witnesses that you two were well into your relationship before the rape charge came up. Sorry to have to burden you with this, but that's what you'll be facing if this goes to trial. Not that I'm not perfectly willing—"

"So Forrest will be dragged through the mud?" Dad asks in a tight voice.

"I don't care," I say. "Let him say whatever he likes. I have the truth on my side."

Ms. Pickett takes a deep breath. "That's easy to *say*..."

"I'm not just saying it. I mean it. I can handle whatever I need to handle."

"What about Scott's past?" Mom asks. "Certainly Forrest isn't the first girl he's taken advantage of."

"Oh, he's got quite a past," Ms. Pickett says. "Drugs, DUIs, even a couple of thefts. But none of that will be admissible, and his family has had enough pull to cushion him from any real consequences. At least so far..."

"I don't want to label anybody," Dad says, "but the way Forrest described him, he sounds like a sociopath—

cold and calculating, manipulative ... I'm terrified for any other girls who find themselves in his path."

Ms. Pickett nods. "I understand. But I saw his videotaped police interview. He's very persuasive ... very charismatic. I'm sure he's had a lot of practice talking his way out of jams."

"Not this one," I say through gritted teeth.

The lawyer considers my words, then nods smartly. "Then we'll move forward. Of course, a grand jury will make the determination of whether the case will proceed, but I can give it our best shot. I just want to make sure you're prepared for what lies ahead."

I lock eyes with Mom: *This is for you too.*

Then I turn back toward Ms. Pickett. "I'm ready."

thirty-four

"Mimosas for everybody!"

Olivia Senior is considerably more perky than the last time she tornadoed through our lives.

She's breezed back into town for our last weekend at the beach. We're sitting on the deck as Dad grills chicken for dinner, and out she prances in a skimpy purple sundress with a pitcher full of yellow-orange beverage, ice cubes tinkling with every flouncy step she takes.

"I bought champagne at the grocery store, and Maureen had orange juice," she prattles. "And I thought, *Hey, we need to celebrate!*"

Dad smiles gamely while Brian and Olivia Junior exchange nervous glances.

"Celebrate *what?*" I ask, wondering if she has any other deep dark family secrets up her sleeve.

"My *grandchild*, of course!" Olivia Senior coos at me.

"Oh, I know I was a little agitated last time I was here, but now that everything's straightened out ... well, we have a baby to celebrate!"

She begins plucking red Solo cups off a stack on the table and pouring mimosas from the pitcher.

"Mom," Olivia says nervously, "you've already had a couple of cocktails ... "

Brian, standing behind her but out of Olivia Senior's line of sight, holds up four fingers and mouths the word for emphasis.

Oh. That explains her good cheer. She's drunk.

"If it's a girl, I want Olivia the Third!" she gushes, handing me a cup only to have it intercepted by Dad.

"Oh, she's a big girl!" Olivia Senior scolds Dad, presumably referring to me. "We're celebrating!"

"She's sixteen," Dad says, trying to sound friendly.

"Well, who the hell is *counting*?"

But Olivia Senior has lost interest in me and is now handing a cup to her daughter.

"I'm pregnant," Olivia tells her in a clipped voice.

"Oh my *god*, you people are uptight," her mother responds, swooping toward Dad and handing him the cup instead. "*You'll* help me celebrate, won't you?" she asks, batting her lashes.

"Sure." He takes a swig and seems to be grateful to have it.

"Will you name her Olivia?" Olivia Senior asks her daughter. "I love our name. I want us to have, like, our own cheerleading squad: the Olivias."

Olivia doesn't even bother to respond as her mother falls into a chair, sloshing a bit of her drink en route.

"Careful," Dad says genially.

"Hey, you are an excellent grill guy," Olivia Senior tells him. "That chicken smells *mmmmm*, it just smells *omigod*, it smells so ... "

"Good?" Dad ventures.

"Yes! *Good!* And you are so sweet to have me, especially considering what a *loon* I was last time I was here. I mean, no big surprise, right, considering my daughter was bawling her eyes out telling me your wife was about to steal her baby, but still, I'm sure I was a little intense when I—"

"Mom," Olivia says softly.

"Hey, it's all good now, baby!" her mother responds, now slurring her words. She gulps the last of her mimosa, then reaches for the pitcher and pours herself another drink.

"*Mom,*" Olivia repeats, but Olivia Senior ignores her.

"Now that we've got all the nasty stuff behind us, we can all be one big happy family, right, Grill Guy? What was your name again? Fred?"

Dad flashes a reluctant smile. "Michael."

"*Michael,*" Olivia Senior repeats, as if it's the most fascinating word that's ever spilled from her gooey-pink lips. "You are a *very nice guy*, Michael. And, you know what, three cheers for you, because from what I can tell, you have been, like, an *excellent* father figure to Brian."

Dad bristles. "I'm Brian's father."

"Yeah, okay, I'll go with that."

"*Mother!*"

Olivia's voice is so shrill now that her mother can't ignore her. "What, baby?" she asks thickly.

"*Shut up,*" Olivia tells her in a clipped voice.

"Hey, the chicken's almost ready," Dad says. "And those Braves... did anyone else catch the last inning of that game? *Unbeliev—*"

"Michael, can I see you and Forrest for a moment?"

We glance at the door leading to the family room. Mom's face looks ashen.

"Sure..." Dad says, signaling Brian to man the grill.

Dad and I walk inside and he closes the door behind us. Mom works her fingers together nervously.

"Diane Pickett just called," she says, staring at her hands.

"Who?" I ask.

"The assistant district attorney," she reminds me.

"Oh." I take a deep breath. "News about Scott?"

Mom looks at me, then stares back down at her hands.

"Yes," she says.

Dad and I exchange glances.

"What is it, Maureen?" he asks.

Mom swallows hard. "Scott was killed in a motorcycle accident last night."

I gasp. "What?"

Mom purses her lips. "He crashed into a pole... no helmet, smelled of liquor..."

"Wow." I lean numbly against the wall.

"That's... it," Mom says after a long pause. "That's it."

I open my mouth, but no words come out. I don't know how to feel. Relieved that I don't have to face him in court? Ecstatic that he'll never hurt another girl? Sad for a family that just lost a son? I'm ... speechless.

Dad puts an arm around me and squeezes me against his side. "That's it," he repeats softly.

We stand there for a few long moments, the wind chimes tinkling on the deck. The sun is just starting to set, an almost crimson sunset tonight. A still, cloudless sunset.

Without even forming the words in my head, I find myself echoing Mom's and Dad's words.

"That's it."

Yes.

That's it.

six months later

"His *head*, his *head*, watch his *head*!"

Olivia winks at me from her hospital bed.

"*Whew*," I say. "I'd have been tempted to roll his head on the floor like a bowling ball if Mom hadn't been here to set me straight."

Mom *tsks* as I settle into a rocking chair with my beautiful nephew, Michael Brian Shepherd III (whose head, just for the record, is still intact), tightening the blanket around his teeny little toes.

He wraps his teeny fingers around my pinkie and stares into my eyes. "He looks just like me," I say dreamily as I examine his exquisitely perfect face.

"He looks like his father," Mom says, and Brian beams from across the room.

"Noooo, you look just like your Aunt Forrest," I say,

falling into Michael Brian's gaze as if his eyes were warm ponds. "Lucky little man."

"I should probably take him..." Mom murmurs, but I swat her away with my free hand.

Oh my god, this baby loves me so much. "He's smiling at me!" I say, and truly, he's either smiling or wincing, or he was for a second there until he scrunched up his perfect little face to try on a new expression.

I make an O with my mouth, and Michael Brian studies me with the intensity of an astronomer discovering a new planet. "Yes, I'm the coolest aunt ever," I coo to him.

Did I mention how alert he is? I know that's, like, the most clichéd thing anybody can say about a newborn, but, OMG, he is off-the-charts alert. I get it now, that whole "he's so alert" observation. And as I hold him, I know one thing for sure: if there is anything on earth I can do to make the world a safer place for him, anything at all, I'll do it in a heartbeat.

"Where's your crazy mom?" I ask Olivia, still soaking in the ponds of perfection that are my nephew's eyes.

"She was actually here for the delivery," Olivia responds.

"Oh. Bummer."

Olivia giggles. "She's on a shopping spree for him now. Brian and I are thinking the guilt card might be just the ticket to avoid having to ever spend a cent on him."

"Yeah, well, tell her to pick up a few things for me unless she wants Michael Brian's favorite aunt schlepping him all over town looking like a homeless person."

"Oh, hush now," Mom scolds us. "That's my grandbaby's grandmother you're talking about. His *other* grandmother."

"The one who doesn't really count," I clarify, and Mom laughs into her fingertips in spite of herself.

"Your mom says he looks like a pianist with his long fingers," Olivia tells me.

"Hmmmm," I muse. "Sounds like you'll have to take him to Mrs. Autry's house soon to try out the piano she's been trying to sell for the past fifteen years."

We all laugh as Mom waves her hand through the air in protest. "Olivia will learn," she says amiably. "She'll learn there's nothing a mother won't do for her baby."

"I learned that nine months ago," Olivia says. "If I was willing to lunge to a toilet twenty times a day for him back then, I'm thinking everything from this point on will be gravy."

"Yeah, good luck with *that* theory," Dad says, and we all laugh, even teeny Michael Brian, and yes, he really *does* seem like he's laughing! Oh ... he's spitting up.

"Puke rag, puke rag," I say, and Mom rushes over with a cloth diaper. She dabs at his teeny, perfect little mouth, then scoops him into her arms despite the fact that he's obviously never been happier in his life than he was in my arms.

"No fair snatching him!" I whine.

"He needs his grandma," Mom says, gazing into the same ponds that just bathed me in warm, velvety wonderfulness.

"It'll be feeding time soon," Brian says, glancing at his watch.

"Ouch, Grandma," Dad teases Mom. "That's one area where you won't come in very handy."

Michael Brian suddenly sneezes, and we all lean in to soak up the moment in appropriate awe.

"Isn't he the most amazing baby ever?" Olivia says, and we gush in agreement.

Yes, we're definitely unanimous: he is the most amazing baby ever.

Glad we got that cleared up.

Nicole Renee Photography

About the Author

Christine Hurley Deriso is an award-winning author of the young adult novel *Then I Met My Sister* and three middle grade novels. She has also contributed to *Ladies' Home Journal*, *Parents*, and other national magazines. Visit her at christinehurleyderiso.com.